INVESTIGATORS

"WE INVESTIGATE ANYTHING"

Jupiter Jones, Founder

Pete Crenshaw, Associate   Bob Andrews, Associate

Jupe is the brain. Pete is the jock. And Bob is Mr. Cool. Together they can solve just about any crime in Rocky Beach, California.

But can they track down a treasure in the Mexican mountains—with nothing to guide them but a stubborn burro?

This sounds like asking for trouble!

THE THREE INVESTIGATORS
C R I M E B U S T E R S

THE 3 INVESTIGATORS

CRIMEBUSTERS™ #5

An Ear
For Danger

by
MARC BRANDEL

based on characters created by Robert Arthur

Borzoi Sprinters
ALFRED A. KNOPF · NEW YORK

DR. M. JERRY WEISS, Distinguished Service Professor of Communications at Jersey City State College, is the educational consultant for Borzoi Sprinters. A past chair of the International Reading Association President's Advisory Committee on Intellectual Freedom, he travels frequently to give workshops on the use of trade books in schools.

A BORZOI SPRINTER PUBLISHED BY ALFRED A. KNOPF, INC.
Copyright © 1989 by Random House, Inc.
All rights reserved under International and Pan-American Copyright Conventions. Published in the United States by Alfred A. Knopf, Inc., New York, and simultaneously in Canada by Random House of Canada Limited, Toronto. Distributed by Random House, Inc., New York.

CRIMEBUSTERS is a trademark of Random House, Inc.

Library of Congress Cataloging-in-Publication Data
Brandel, Marc.
An ear for danger.
(The 3 investigators. Crimebusters ; #5)
"A Borzoi sprinter."
Summary: A vacation trip to Mexico for the Three Investigators, now age seventeen, turns into an unexpected quest for treasure in the Sierra Madre.
ISBN 0-394-89943-1 (pbk.)
[1. Mystery and detective stories] I. Arthur, Robert.
II. Title. III. Series.
PZ7.B7362Ear 1989 [Fic] 88-45880

RL: 5.1
Also available in a library edition from Random House, Inc.—
ISBN 0-394-99943-6

Manufactured in the United States of America
10 9 8 7 6 5 4 3 2 1

1

A Real Puzzler

"THIS IS RIDICULOUS," JUPITER JONES SAID. "A KID OF ten could solve this puzzle."

The seventeen-year-old didn't want to sound conceited in front of his two friends, so he didn't add that he thought he could have solved it himself at age five.

Pete Crenshaw, who was working on another copy of the same crossword, didn't think it was so easy. Would a kid of ten know who "Dagwood's wife" was? The name Dagwood did sound familiar to him, but he couldn't quite place it.

Bob Andrews propped his long legs up on the desk. He had solved the Dagwood clue. He penciled in the answer and moved on to the next one. "Frivolous or light-headed." Five letters beginning with G. "Giddy."

The Three Investigators were sitting in their headquarters in The Jones Salvage Yard in Rocky Beach, California, a small town a few miles up the Coast Highway from Los Angeles.

They were into the second week of their summer

vacation. Ordinarily, they would all have been busy outdoors. Their detective firm had no cases right now, but the guys had plenty of other things to do.

Ordinarily Jupe—as Jupiter was known to his friends—would have been swimming in the ocean. A brisk swim every day kept your weight down. He hoped.

Pete would have been surfing or driving his girlfriend, Kelly Madigan, around in the MG convertible he had bought secondhand and spent weeks souping up.

Bob would have been at an outdoor rock concert. Probably with one or two or three of the girls who followed him around like groupies. He worked parttime for a local talent agent and could often get free tickets. Actually Bob's quiet good looks were far more attractive to his string of female admirers than any freebies.

But for the past three days the TV weatherman had kept forecasting scattered showers. As far as Jupe could see, that meant it would only drizzle as long as you stayed indoors. If you went out in the open, you were in for a good soaking.

He wrote in another two letters and threw his pen down beside the completed crossword puzzle.

" 'Opposite of down,' " he said contemptuously. "Give me a break! A gerbil could guess these answers."

"I did get that one." Pete smiled. "Up."

Jupe picked up the leaflet on which the puzzle was printed and glanced at the instructions on the back.

" 'This contest is open only to male high school students between the ages of fourteen and eighteen,' " he read aloud. " 'There is no entrance fee.' " He looked up. "Where did you get these things, Pete?"

"They were giving them away at the supermarket here in town," Pete explained. "The answers are easy for you, Jupe. You were born with an overgrown brain. But what's 'sorrow or misfortune'? Three letters ending in E."

"Woe," Bob told him.

Jupe went back to reading the instructions.

" 'The grand prize is an all-expenses-paid, two-week visit to a beautiful ranch in northern Mexico. Attractions there include horseback riding, fishing in the large fresh-water lake, camping, delicious barbe-cued steaks—' "

"Stop right there," Pete put in. "I'll take it!" He was the most athletic of the teenage detectives and had a healthy appetite.

He looked up at the ceiling of the trailer that served the Investigators as headquarters. Raindrops pinged on the metal roof.

"And maybe the weather's better in Mexico than it is here," Pete added. "I don't mind surfing in the rain. But how can you surf when there's no waves? The ocean's as flat as a football field."

Jupe hadn't been listening to Pete or the raindrops. He was still absorbed in the instructions on the back of the leaflet.

" 'No answers should be submitted in writing,' " he

continued reading aloud. " 'They must be recorded on tape. First read the answers to the across clues into your tape recorder—' "

He broke off. His eyes moved rapidly down the rest of the page.

"That's weird," he said.

"What's weird?" Bob asked. The instructions seemed simple enough to him. As simple as the answer to "Not there."

"Here," he wrote in before glancing up at Jupe.

"Printing leaflets costs money," Jupiter mused. "Two weeks on a ranch in Mexico costs money too. Why would anyone put up all that dough for such a dumb contest?"

"Because it's an advertising gimmick," Bob told him. The pop music world in which he spent so much of his spare time had taught him to recognize a come-on when he saw one. "They want you to buy a tape recorder. And a blank cassette."

Jupe nodded. "Makes sense," he agreed. "Only there's no mention of a store where you can buy them. No word about any brand names either."

"They were handing out the leaflets at the supermarket," Pete reminded him. "Maybe they've got a sale on stuff like that or something."

Jupe shook his head. "If you had eyes for anything besides Kelly Madigan," he told Pete, "you might have noticed they don't stock any electronic equipment at the Rocky Beach supermarket. Not even pocket calculators."

He looked at the leaflet again.

Jupe, who was short and overweight, did not enjoy moving more than he had to. Two weeks on a ranch in Mexico, riding horses and fishing, was not his idea of a grand prize. But the puzzle contest had stirred his curiosity. Who was putting up the money for it? And why?

"They've probably been distributing these leaflets all over the Los Angeles area," Jupe said. "And the answers are so obvious they're going to get hundreds of perfect solutions. So they'll have to pick one. At least there are three of us. Together, we have three times as good a chance of winning."

Bob looked at him in surprise. "You mean you want to audition for this gig?" he asked.

"Sure. Why not?" Jupe frowned. Bob's habit of using the slang of musicians sometimes got under his skin. Though Bob had drifted away from the Three Investigators into the fringes of show business, Jupe was as committed to The Team as ever.

Jupe took a tape recorder out of his desk drawer, inserted a blank cassette, and handed it to Pete with his own completed puzzle.

"You go first," he said. "Start with the horizontal words."

Pete glanced at the crossword before switching on the recorder. He made a disgusted sound.

"*That's* the answer to 'If you do this, you won't go'? 'Come'? Why can't they just say 'Opposite of go'?" He shook his head.

An hour later the Three Investigators had three correct, recorded tapes packed into manila envelopes made out to the Santa Monica address printed on the leaflets. They had also included their names and addresses as mentioned in the instructions.

The sound of raindrops on the roof had stopped.

"Might as well go out and mail them," Bob said, "before it starts pouring again." He had taken out his contact lenses and was busy cleaning them with his special kit.

"Or we could drive into Santa Monica," Jupe suggested, "and deliver them by hand."

"What's in Santa Monica?" Pete wanted to know. "Besides a lot of wet beach."

"We could ride around for a while," Bob told him. "Maybe stop for a pizza. Check out the action. See what shows up." He put his lenses back into his eyes.

Pete nodded. He was hungry.

Jupe didn't say anything. He had sworn off fast food. It was fattening. And he knew what would show up: girls.

Not that Jupe had anything against girls. He was as interested in them as either of his two friends. The trouble was, they didn't seem interested in him. Especially when Bob was around.

But Jupe did want to go into Santa Monica. He wanted to scout out the address on the crossword puzzle leaflet. A sign on the door might give him some lead as to what the contest was all about.

"Okay, let's go," he said.

"Whose car do we take?" Pete wanted to know. "The roof of my MG leaks and I haven't had time to fix it."

"Well, we definitely can't take my car," Jupiter said darkly. His Honda Civic had been totaled while the Three Investigators were working on a case. And his savings were still too meager to pay for another car.

"Ugh," Pete groaned, "squashed in the bug again."

Bob socked him in the arm as the three guys headed for Bob's red Volkswagen. Jupe sat in front while Bob drove. Pete slumped in the back with his feet up on the seat. At seventeen, Pete was six foot one with legs to match. There was no way he could sit in the front of the VW without bruising his knees on the dashboard.

It was drizzling again as they drove down the Coast Highway.

"It's abnormal," Pete complained, looking out at the rain-washed shore.

"Yeah." Bob knew what Pete meant. "Not like San Francisco. You expect it to rain there." His job had taken him up there a few times. His boss, Sax Sendler, had used Bob as a roadie for groups he booked in that city.

Once in Santa Monica the Three Investigators soon found the street they were looking for in the downtown shopping area. Jupe watched the numbers go by.

"There," he said suddenly, touching Bob's arm. "Just up ahead where all those people . . ."

He didn't need to say any more. A crowd had

gathered outside one of the stores on the street. Two police cars with circling lights were drawn up at the curb.

"Come on." Jupe opened his door as Bob brought the VW to a stop.

"That's it!" Jupe told them. "The address we're supposed to mail our entries to. Let's find out what's going on."

The three friends edged their way into the crowd. Two policemen were rattling the glass-topped door, peering inside. They were evidently preparing to break in if they saw anything suspicious.

Jupe studied the building in his usual methodical way. It was impossible to tell what the store had once sold. It didn't sell anything now. The plate glass display windows had all been whitewashed on the inside. FOR SALE signs were plastered all over them.

None of the people Jupe asked seemed to know what was happening. But he could tell one thing. If anyone had been trying to break into the shop, they hadn't succeeded in opening the door. Maybe the burglar alarm had gone off before they could get inside.

He walked across the street to a drugstore and bought some stamps from a machine. He dropped the three manila envelopes holding the tapes into a nearby mailbox. Then he rejoined the crowd outside the empty store, looking for his two friends.

He saw Bob at once. The tall, blond guy was talking to a pretty, dark-haired girl about his own age near the police car. She was a nose wrinkler, Jupe noticed. She couldn't say ten words without wrinkling her nose. But he had to admit that she was also very cute.

Pete reappeared, and waited impatiently with Jupe for Bob to finish. Finally the third Investigator touched the girl's arm in a friendly way and left her. All three guys climbed back into the VW.

"She give you her phone number?" Jupe asked a little enviously as they drove away.

Bob shook his head.

"She collects early Judy Garland records," he explained. "She's not my type."

Maybe that explained the nose wrinkling, Jupe thought. The girl had copied it from late-night Judy Garland movies on TV.

"How come it took you ten minutes to find out she didn't like rock?" Pete asked as they headed back to the Coast Highway. "I thought you were a fast worker."

"That was just for openers," Bob told him. "The rest of the time she was talking about the burglary. Attempted burglary, anyway."

"So give," Jupe said. They were supposed to be investigating the puzzles, not picking up girls.

"The way she told it," Bob went on, "she was coming out of the coffee shop across the street when the burglar alarm outside that store went off. Then she saw a woman run away from the store, jump into a blue car, and burn rubber driving away."

"Did she see the woman's face?" Jupe asked.

"Blond hair. Slender build. About forty years old,"

Bob said. "Color of eyes—unknown. The woman was wearing shades."

"Shades!" Pete exclaimed. "On a day like this you'd need windshield wipers on 'em!"

"Yeah," Jupe agreed. "Our forty-year-old blonde sounds like a bit of a mystery."

He was silent for a moment, thinking it over.

"She tries to break into an empty store—to find what?"

Silence.

Jupe couldn't let it go. "Something so valuable that she risked arrest to get it. Guys, there's more to this contest than barbecued steaks!"

2

Down Mexico Way

THE FOLLOWING DAY THE WEATHER CLEARED. THE usually reliable California sun shone again. For the next three weeks the Three Investigators were all busy in their own ways.

Bob was putting in more time at his job. His boss, Sax Sendler of Rock-Plus, Inc., talent agency, had booked several of his groups for a big outdoor rock concert. Bob was working twelve hours a day, preparing advance publicity and running errands and helping to set up the equipment.

Pete was having trouble with his girlfriend, Kelly. She seemed to have cooled off a little lately. Although Kelly was the one who had first suggested going steady, her way of going steady wasn't what it had been. Sometimes when he'd arranged to pick her up at her house, he'd find she wasn't home. She had gone shopping with a girlfriend. This hadn't changed Pete's feelings about her. And he often felt she was just as attached to him as ever, in her own casual way. But Pete did find he was wasting a lot of his vacation waiting around for her. It cut into his surfing time and even his karate practice.

Jupe was again making a determined effort to lose weight. At 5 feet 8¾ inches and 190 pounds, he could no longer hide the truth from himself. He wasn't just stocky. He was . . . well, maybe not exactly *fat*. But his physique could use a lot of improvement. His problem was that the more he swam and practiced his judo, the hungrier he felt. And the harder it was to stick to his new diet.

This week it was Keil Halfebrot's Body-Building Regimen—nothing but protein and salads. Since muscleman Halfebrot looked like Superman and Jupiter resembled a large pear, he thought it would be worth a shot.

One afternoon Jupe was standing outside his electronics workshop, next to Headquarters. The workshop was a tinkerer's paradise, jammed with all the equipment needed to build and repair the electronic gadgets the team used on their cases.

And that's exactly what Jupiter was doing now—tinkering. He was testing a new security device for the workshop, a lock that could only be opened when he spoke the special password.

Pete was on the other side of the headquarters trailer in his makeshift auto shop. He had been stood up by Kelly for the second time that week.

Jupe adjusted a final silicon chip.

"Beware of the dog," he commanded.

"What?" Pete kept cutting the canvas that would become a new roof for his convertible.

"Rats," Jupe complained. "The lock's supposed to open when I say that. *Beware of the dog,*" he repeated louder. Pete sauntered over. "First it's rats, now it's dogs," he commented. "Make up your mind."

As Jupiter was rolling his eyes the phone rang in his workshop. Jupe ignored it, knowing there was another extension in Headquarters. Bob was inside, laying out a leaflet for the rock concert on the word processor. The call was probably one of his girlfriends begging him for a date. Let him answer the phone.

After a moment it stopped ringing. Pete went back to his auto pit.

Bob stepped out of the trailer. "Jupe, it's your Aunt Mathilda." Jupe caught a glimpse of three pretty young faces inside before his friend closed the door.

"She wants to talk to me?" Jupe asked, a little surprised.

His Aunt Mathilda and his Uncle Titus had given him a home since he was four years old, when his parents were killed in an automobile accident. Jupe was still grateful for that, and he was fond of both Titus and Mathilda. But now that he was seventeen, they no longer played the important part in his life they once had.

A few years ago summonses from Aunt Mathilda had been as frequent as homework assignments. They had usually meant one thing—work. She had endless jobs for him to do in the salvage yard. But recently

Jupe had computerized the inventory in exchange for freedom from those chores. So a call from Aunt Mathilda these days was as rare as girlfriends for Jupe.

"No. She just had a message for you," Bob said. "There's someone over at the house who wants to talk to you."

"Who?" Jupe asked.

"Name of Rice." Bob smiled. "Something to do with that puzzle contest you auditioned for."

"Yeah?" Jupe felt his interest rise. He hadn't forgotten about the crossword contest. He never forgot anything. But he had been so busy trying to lose weight that he hadn't thought much about it lately.

Now he might have a chance to find out who was putting up the dough for those two weeks in Mexico. The Three Investigators decided they all should meet Mr. Rice. They were crossing the road outside the junkyard when a man appeared on the porch of the Jones house.

He was tall and lean. In his late thirties, Jupe guessed. And he looked like quite a dude in his designer jeans and hand-tooled cowboy boots. He had an expensive Stetson cocked at an angle on his head. As the Investigators approached him he took it off and waved it in greeting.

"Hi. I'm Dustin Rice."

He looked at the three guys in turn. "So which of you is the lucky one?" he asked. "No, don't tell me. See if I can guess."

He turned to Pete and smiled at him. "Just for fun,

let me hear your voice, friend. Say . . ." He hesitated. "Say, 'South of the border, down Mexico way.' "

"South of the border, down Mexico way," Pete obliged him grudgingly. He wasn't much taken with Dustin Rice.

Rice shook his head. He waved his Stetson at Bob. "Now you."

"Mouth of disorder, brown Mexico day," Bob said. He had never liked the song anyway, and he didn't feel like taking orders from this cowboy.

Dustin Rice managed to keep smiling. He looked at Jupe. Jupe looked back at him.

His first impression of this man was that he was slightly unreal. His jaunty smile and breezy manner weren't altogether convincing. He reminded Jupe of someone walking a tightrope, carefully planning his next step.

"Would you mind letting me hear you say it?" he asked Jupe.

"South of the border, down Mexico way."

The effect was astonishing. Rice's eyes brightened with excitement. He stepped forward and shook Jupe's hand.

"My friends call me Dusty," he said. "You must be Jupiter Jones and your aunt says they call you Jupe. It's my great pleasure to tell you you've won the grand prize in my crossword puzzle contest! A free visit to my ranch." His smile broadened. "Down Mexico way. And I'm looking forward to having you there as my guest, Jupe, and . . ."

His voice trailed away. Jupe was holding up his hand like a traffic cop at a busy intersection.

Given his height and weight, Jupe was not a naturally imposing figure. But he had the remarkable ability of asserting his authority when he felt like it.

He felt like it now. He wasn't going to let Dustin Rice take it for granted that the dream of Jupe's life was to spend two weeks on a Mexican ranch hopping on and off horses. He had some questions he wanted answered first.

He said so.

"Shoot," Dusty agreed. "Ask me anything you like."

"How many other people won this grand prize?"

"None. Only you. You were the only winner."

"I was the only one who got all the answers right?"

Dusty hesitated a second. "Sure," he said.

Jupe nodded thoughtfully. He knew that was a lie. Pete and Bob had sent in exactly the same answers as he had. Why was Dusty holding back the real reason Jupe had been chosen as the winner? And why couldn't a girl enter or win? The Investigator tucked those questions away in his mind. They'd be answered later when he had more information.

"Where's the money coming from?" he asked next. "Who's paying for everything?"

"I am."

"What for?"

"Publicity. Publicity for my ranch." Dustin Rice put his Stetson back on. It seemed to give him more confidence. "I'm planning to turn the place into a summer camp for guys like you. And I'm hoping to get a good write-up about the contest in the Sunday papers."

That did make some sense to Jupe. Barely.

He was about to go on with his questions, but his attention was distracted for a moment. A blue car, a Chevy, was approaching the house. It slowed as it came nearer and at first Jupe thought it was going to stop. Then it suddenly gained speed again and drove out of sight. The sun had been shining on the windshield and Jupe hadn't been able to see the driver clearly. He *had* made out that it was a woman. A woman with blond hair, wearing dark glasses.

He turned back to Dusty.

"If I accept this grand prize," he said, "is it okay if my two friends here come with me?"

Dusty frowned. "You mean I'd have to pay their expenses too?" he asked.

"Yeah, that's exactly what I mean," Jupe said firmly.

Dusty took off his Stetson and thoughtfully twisted the brim. He began to talk about bus fares, food at the ranch . . .

Jupe let him talk. He had already made up his mind to turn down the prize unless Pete and Bob were included. This puzzle contest was becoming a promising case for the Three Investigators. And the Three Investigators were a team.

Dusty was still going on about money, adding up how much more everything would cost if Jupe's friends . . .

"Then I'm afraid you'll have to give the prize to somebody else," Jupe interrupted him.

Dusty shifted his feet, looking down at his hand-tooled boots.

"You win, big guy," he agreed. "I guess I can swing it."

Bob reached out and touched Jupe's arm. "Let's take ten," he suggested. He walked off the porch, followed by his two friends.

"You really want to do this, Jupe?" he asked as soon as they were out of hearing.

Jupe did. The thought of not pursuing this case was agony to him. "Absolutely," he said. "Something really weird is going on if this guy is willing to pay for *three* vacations. Don't you want to know why?"

"Well . . ." Bob had been working so hard these past few weeks, he felt he could do with a change of scene. Sax would be leaving on a trip to Hawaii as soon as the rock concert was over. There would be nothing to keep Bob in California while his boss was away. He'd just miss a few of his karate lessons.

"Okay," he said. "Deal me in. Anytime after the concert Thursday night."

Jupe and Bob both looked at Pete. It was up to him now.

"I don't know," Pete said. "I'm kind of afraid that if I leave town, Kelly might forget all about me."

"She might miss you, too," Bob pointed out.

"Yeah, maybe." Pete remembered a line he had once seen on a greeting card: "Absence makes the heart grow fonder." The idea of Kelly with a fonder heart, a Kelly who would never stand him up again, was very appealing.

"Oh, okay," he said. "I guess I can keep sending her cards and things so she'll know I'm still alive."

Dustin Rice couldn't hide his relief when the Three Investigators returned to the porch and told him they had decided to accept his grand prize.

He gave them a map of northern Mexico, showing them how to get to Lareto, the town nearest to his ranch. After a bit of haggling, he also handed over six hundred dollars in cash for their expenses on the trip. Dusty gave them his phone number so they could call him once they crossed the border. He would pick them up in Lareto. The three guys watched the rancher climb into his Jeep with its Mexican plates. Then they went back to their tasks in the junkyard.

Early the next morning Jupe made his usual trip to the mailbox at the bottom of the drive. Uncle Titus always got what he jokingly called "junk" mail— notices of sales of scrap metal and other junk he might want to buy for his salvage yard.

Jupe sorted through it until he came to a manila envelope. He could feel something hard and rectangular inside it. It was addressed to Mr. Jupiter Jones and had no address and no stamp. It had been delivered by hand.

He took it back to Headquarters and opened it. Inside the envelope was a tape cassette. Nothing else. No writing on the tape label to explain what it was.

Jupe fitted it into his recorder and hit the play button. He heard only a long silence as the tape unwound. Then finally a male voice spoke clearly and urgently.

"Please don't come to Mexico," the voice said. "You'll be in terrible danger if you do. Please, please, don't come down here. Stay in California and—"

The voice suddenly cut off.

That was all. Jupe played the tape to the end. He heard nothing else but silence.

He sat back in his swivel chair. The message was disturbing enough in itself. "You'll be in terrible danger . . ." But something else about it puzzled and worried him. He couldn't help feeling he'd heard that voice before. It was somehow weirdly familiar.

When Pete drove up next to Headquarters a few minutes later, Jupe asked him to listen to the tape. After explaining where he had found it, he played it straight through.

To Jupiter's surprise, Pete began smiling. "Is this some kind of joke, Jupe?" he asked.

"A joke?"

"Sending yourself scary messages."

"I didn't send it. I told you. I found it in the mailbox."

"Then someone's doing a great job of imitating your voice."

"*My* voice?"

"Sure." Pete picked up the recorder. "I'd bet my MG that was *you* talking on that tape, Jupe."

3

Alive on Arrival

JUPITER SAT BY THE WINDOW IN THE BATTERED OLD bus watching Mexico roll by.

The Three Investigators had originally planned to drive down in Pete's convertible. But a call to AAA had warned Pete that unleaded gas was hard to find in Mexico. Leaded gas would wreck the MG's catalytic converter, and Pete would have to get a new one before he could legally drive the car in California again. That would cost at least three hundred dollars.

"No way," Pete decided. "I'm going to need all my dough to take Kelly out when I get back. So she'll be glad to see me."

He had also refused to travel several hundred miles sandwiched in the back of Bob's VW bug. In the end the three guys had decided to accept Dusty's suggestion and take advantage of the cheap Mexican bus fares.

Jupe was wearing a new T-shirt. It said HELLO, I'M FRIENDLY in Spanish. He hoped it would encourage strangers to talk to him so he could practice his own fairly good Spanish.

21

He twisted on the hard plastic seat to look back at the other two Investigators. Bob was reading the paperback history of Mexico he had brought with him. A stunningly pretty Mexican girl had found a place beside him. Naturally. She kept glancing at Bob as though she hoped he'd stop reading and talk to her.

Pete had somehow managed to fit his long legs under the seat in front of him and was fast asleep.

Both of them were wearing new T-shirts too. Bob's said THE SURVIVORS, the name of one of the rock groups Sax Sendler handled.

Pete's T-shirt had KELLY MADIGAN printed on it. Kelly had given it to him as a going-away present so he wouldn't forget *her*. That had surprised Pete. It seemed to mean she wouldn't forget him either.

Jupe glanced at the woman sitting behind Bob. She didn't look any different from any of the other Mexican countrywomen on the bus. She was brown-skinned and dressed in a cotton blouse and wool skirt. Two long black pigtails dangled below the purple shawl she wore over her head. Jupe had first noticed her in the bus station in Santa Monica. And although they had already changed buses twice after crossing the border, she was still traveling with them.

Bob had put down his book and was enjoying a talk with the pretty young Mexican girl next to him. He was glad to find she spoke English.

"I'm afraid my Spanish is lousy," he apologized. "Just *buenas días* and stuff like that."

"How do you like Mexico?" she asked.

"I think it's great."

"Why?"

"Well . . ." Bob thought about it. "In the States it's like one of those big bands. Everyone knows their part and has their own sheet music. You can kind of tell what's coming up next."

"And in Mexico?" she prompted him with a smile.

"It's more like a jam session. Everybody taking off and doing their own thing. Not just the way they drive down here. But the way the bus keeps stopping in the middle of nowhere and a bunch of people just disappear into the desert."

"They're going to their farms," she explained. "And they may have to walk five miles from the road."

"But they don't seem to mind," Bob said. "They set off smiling and talking together. Like they were going to their own private party."

"Maybe you're right." She nodded thoughtfully. "I lived for several years in America. Life is much easier there. But people do seem more cheerful in Mexico."

The bus lurched to a stop in a small town. Jupe glanced at his map, then signaled to Pete and Bob. They had to change buses again.

Bob said good-bye to the Mexican girl as he took his tote bag down from the rack. The bus station was a small café in a busy street. The three friends hurried into it.

"Boy, am I starved!" Pete exclaimed as they sat down at a table.

Pete and Bob ordered beef burritos with rice and

beans. Jupe hesitated. He wasn't going to be able to stick to his new diet in Mexico. Dusty had warned them not to eat salads or uncooked vegetables on the trip. But rice and beans! That was like begging to put *on* weight.

He ate two chicken tacos. Chicken was less fatty than beef. And tortillas had less starch in them than bread—he hoped. But the chicken was heavily flavored with chili peppers.

"Argh!" Jupe said as the three guys left the café to catch their bus. "My tongue feels like it's on fire."

As Jupe walked toward the bus a man in a torn leather jacket suddenly stepped in front of him. He was tall, heavily built, about twenty years old. He put his hand on Jupe's chest and pushed him back roughly. "No room," he said in Spanish. "No room for you on this bus."

The three guys exchanged surprised looks. The Mexicans they had seen so far had seemed so friendly.

Jupe could see half the seats on the bus were still empty. Using his most polite Spanish, he explained this to the Mexican.

The man gave him another, harder push. It felt like a punch in the chest this time.

"No," he said. "Go away. Get out of here. You and your friends go back to the United States. We don't want you here."

"I'm not going back to the United States," Jupe stated firmly in Spanish. "I'm taking this bus. Please get out of my way."

Instead of stepping aside, the man in the leather jacket grabbed Jupe by the shoulder and drew him close.

"Get lost," he said. "Or I'll beat your brains out."

Jupe had been practicing his judo particularly hard these past few weeks in his effort to lose weight. He was getting quite good at it. But he didn't think he was any match for this hefty young Mexican. Before he could get a hold on him, the man would knock out several of his teeth. He quickly freed his shoulder from the other's grip and stepped back to avoid the blow.

Pete and Bob had been trying to follow the Spanish, but Pete had no trouble understanding exactly what was happening now. He moved up beside Jupe.

"What's going on?" he asked.

Jupe explained that the man in the leather jacket didn't want to let them on the bus.

"Why not?"

"Search me. Maybe he just doesn't like Yankees."

"Gotcha," Pete said cheerfully.

Moving lightly on the balls of his feet, he started past the young man. The Mexican swung at him. If his fist had landed on Pete's face, it would have knocked him flat. It never reached him. As the man struck, Pete hit him hard just below the shoulder with a knife-hand strike, the *shuto-uchi*. The leather-covered arm stopped in midswing as though paralyzed. Then it fell slowly to the man's side. He grabbed his own shoulder with his other hand and faced Pete.

Pete waited, his legs slightly bent, his hands flat in the ready posture.

The Mexican looked at him, startled. He was still gripping his own shoulder, trying to knead some life back into it.

Pete raised his right hand, ready to chop at him again.

The man shook his head. "Okay," he muttered in Spanish. "Okay. Enough. I'm not going to get my neck broken. Not even for a *million* pesos."

He was still shaking his head as he walked away.

At that moment Jupe burped. The tension broke as Bob and Pete hooted with laughter. Jupe's face burned.

"Chicken tacos staging a comeback?" Bob teased.

"Hey, let's move it," Pete said. "Our bus is ready to go."

The Three Investigators climbed onto the bus. They hadn't seen the woman with the purple shawl in the café. But there she was again in a back seat.

They watched her take several peso bills out of her purse and hand them out the window beside her. A brown hand reached up and grabbed them. As the hand closed over the money, the guys caught a glimpse of the sleeve of a leather jacket.

They settled into their seats as the bus started forward.

It was the last leg of their long trip. All three guys fell into an uneasy doze that lasted all night. They found it difficult to sleep much. Every village they passed through had concrete mounds a foot high stretching right across the main street. The bumps kept people from driving too fast through the town—and from sleeping on buses.

They arrived in Lareto around nine o'clock in the morning. The bus stopped in a small square with trees and benches grouped around a bandstand.

The guys had phoned Dusty from the border. He was waiting for them in his Jeep, obviously pleased to see them. But he seemed strangely impatient, too. As he helped them stow their bags in the Jeep, he kept saying it wouldn't be long before they got to the ranch—as though it couldn't be too soon to suit him.

As they drove out of the square, Jupe turned and looked behind him.

The woman in the purple shawl was standing on the sidewalk staring after them. Jupe waved at her in a friendly way. She didn't wave back.

He couldn't blame her for being sore at them. The way he figured it, she had given several thousand pesos to that Mexican in the leather jacket to stop the Three Investigators from getting to Lareto.

And here they were.

4

A Blonde for Jupe

THEY DROVE FOR TWO HOURS BEFORE THEY REACHED the ranch. Most of the time they were on a dirt road that wound up through wooded hills. Ahead of them in the distance they kept glimpsing a range of tall mountains. Dusty explained they were part of the Sierra Madre.

That reminded Bob of an old movie he had seen on television. "That's where Humphrey Bogart and his pals found the treasure of the Sierra Madre, isn't it?" he asked with a smile.

Dusty didn't seem to realize Bob was kidding. He shook his head seriously. *"The Treasure of the Sierra Madre* was just a movie," he said. "There's no treasure in those mountains."

Bob made a face at Pete in the back seat.

Soon after that they reached the ranch. The ranch house was a long, low wooden building standing in open grassland that sloped down to a lake. The only signs of life were some horses grazing in an open field.

Pete looked at the lake. He guessed it was about two

or three miles long and maybe half a mile wide.
Should be a great place for fishing, he thought, glad
he had brought his rod and tackle with him. He
couldn't see any houses on the other side of the lake,
only a clump of trees. But way beyond the trees he
could make out what looked like the tower of an old
church. So probably people did live over there.

Dusty led the way across the porch and into a large,
pleasant room with an open fireplace and comfortable
chairs.

"I guess you're hungry, aren't you?" he asked.

"You've read my mind," Pete agreed. Dusty clapped
his hands and almost immediately a Mexican man
appeared through the archway at the end of the room.

"This is Ascención," Dusty said. "He's the cook
around here." He didn't bother to introduce the three
visitors by their names.

Ascención was about fifty, sturdily built, with a
deep brown craggy face and straight black hair. He was
wearing cowboy boots and jeans and a denim shirt. He
looked more like a ranch hand than a cook, Jupe
thought.

Dusty spoke rapidly to him in Spanish. Jupe caught
the words "breakfast" and "at once." Ascención nodded. His brown eyes were so dark, they looked almost
black. Bob noticed that he never looked directly at
Dusty. The tension between them reminded him of
rival rock stars.

Ascención was a great cook. He soon brought in a
big platter of ham and eggs, hashbrowns, and hot

rolls. Pete and Bob settled down to everything with healthy appetites. Jupe stuck to the ham and eggs. Proteins were okay with Keil Halfebrot. Carbohydrates were the killers.

Dusty sat at the long table with them but didn't eat anything. He kept picking the dough out of a roll in a nervous way. He seemed to be waiting for his three guests to finish so he could get on with something. Something that was worrying him.

"Had enough?" he asked as soon as Pete had swallowed his last mouthful.

"Yeah. It was great," Pete said. He could have eaten another whole plateful, but Dusty had already started toward the door.

"Come on," he called. "I'll show you over the ranch."

Outside, he quickly led the way around the end of the house to a wide fenced-in field. On one side of the field was a small wooden shed.

"Like to see my burro," Dusty said. He wasn't asking them. He hurried the three guys toward the shed. Before they reached it a small donkey, what Mexicans call a burro, stumbled out of the shed and skittered shyly away from them.

Except for a black line down its back and across its shoulders, it was so light-skinned it was almost white. It had huge ears, which it kept twitching nervously, and a long tufted tail. Its front legs had been hobbled with a rope so that, although it seemed anxious to run away, it could move only with short, unsteady steps.

Pete, who liked all animals on sight, started quickly forward. He held out his hand to pat the burro's neck. Dusty stopped him.

"Don't touch her and don't say anything," he told the three guys in a low, urgent voice. "She's very young. Less than two years old. And she hasn't been tamed yet."

The burro had managed to get several yards away by then. She kicked out suddenly with her hind legs as though warning them not to come any closer.

"Quite a lot of wild burros live in the mountains. This one strayed onto my land a couple of months ago and I decided to keep her," Dusty explained. "I call her Blondie. You can guess why."

He looked at Pete. "You can try calling her now if you like," he said. "Just say, 'Come here, Blondie.' Let's see what she does."

Here he goes again, Pete thought resentfully, telling us what to say like we were third graders. But Pete really liked the little animal, so he played along.

"Come here, Blondie," he called in a gentle voice. "Come here."

The burro laid her long ears back so that they were almost touching her neck. Pete knew from his experience with horses that this meant Blondie was wary. Or angry. He called her again, but all she did was hobble a few more feet away from him.

"You try," Dusty told Bob.

"What for?" Bob shrugged. "All I'll get is the same put-down from her."

"Maybe you're right." Dusty did his best to smile. He looked at Jupe. "You mind trying to call her for me?" he asked politely.

Jupe could take animals or leave them. He didn't care if the burro came to him or not. But he could tell from the worried look in Dusty's eyes, the way the rancher suddenly gripped Jupe's arm, that this mattered a lot to Dusty. Jupe was curious.

He freed his arm. "Come here, Blondie," he called in a bored voice.

The effect was astonishing. The burro's head swung around instantly. She looked straight at Jupe. Her ears twitched once and then pointed forward.

"I don't believe it!" Pete said.

"Again!" Dusty whispered excitedly. "Say it again!"

"Come here, Blondie." This time Jupe's voice sounded a bit more interested.

The burro strained against the rope that hobbled her front legs and ambled toward Jupe as quickly as she could. She stopped less than a foot away from him. Stretching her neck, she prodded his chest gently with her nose.

"She's fallen for you!" Bob said, slapping his friend on the back. "How do you do it, Jupe? Three little words and she's crazy about you."

Jupe stepped back. The burro's response to him had caught him by surprise. And Bob's kidding made him feel embarrassed.

"Stroke her." Dusty was gripping his arm again. "See what happens if you touch her."

Out of sheer curiosity, Jupe stretched out his hand and stroked Blondie's neck. Her ears stood straight up. She rubbed her nose against Jupe's chest again.

Dusty let go of Jupe's arm. He was smiling like a man who had just won first prize in a quiz show.

"I bet she'd even let you ride her," Dusty said. "Go on. It's okay. Even at her age, she's a very strong little animal. She can carry you. Easily."

Jupe hesitated. He didn't particularly want to ride the burro. But Dusty's excitement had started a whole train of questions in his mind. Something was going on here that he didn't understand. As an Investigator, he had to follow every possible lead.

He swung his right leg over the burro's back and settled astride her. Blondie turned her head and tried to look up at him with her huge soft eyes. Her ears were bolt upright. She seemed to like the idea of having Jupe as her jockey.

"Say, giddyup," Dusty whispered urgently.

The words stirred a sudden memory in Jupe's mind.

"Giddyup," he said. "Giddyup, Blondie."

He had to hold on to the burro's neck to keep his balance as she clumsily ambled forward. Memory had given him a clue. He decided to try a little experiment.

"Whoa, Blondie," he said. "Whoa!"

The burro obediently came to a stop.

"Well, she certainly seems to have taken a shine to you," Dusty told Jupe as he got off the burro's back.

"Yeah, it's your animal magnetism, Jupe," Pete put in. "That'll do it with blondes every time."

"Very funny," Jupe said. "Maybe I remind her of somebody." He was looking at Dusty.

"How could you?" Dusty shook his head. "That burro was quite wild when she strayed down here. The only people she's ever known in her life are me and Ascención. And you don't look anything like either of us."

"No, I don't *look* like you," Jupe admitted. He reached up and pinched his lower lip. It was a habit he had when he was trying to figure something out. He claimed it helped him to think.

He was still pinching it half an hour later as he sat on his bunk in the large, comfortable room he was sharing with his two friends. Looking out the window, he could see the field with the shed in it. The white burro was standing close to the fence. She looked toward the house and brayed softly, as though calling to Jupe, wanting him to come back and stroke her again.

"Blondie!" Pete, who was assembling his fishing rod, said suddenly. "Dagwood's wife. In the comic strip. 'Blondie' was one of the answers in that crossword puzzle."

"Yeah, it was," Jupe agreed. "But it isn't just Blondie. There are the other clues too."

"What other clues?" Bob was unpacking his tote bag. He folded his spare jeans neatly away in a drawer. "Clues to why this blonde finds you irresistible?"

Jupe ignored him. "The words Dusty asked us to say to that little burro just now. They were all answers in that crossword puzzle."

"Yeah?" Pete said. "Which ones?"

Jupe leaned back against the wall and half closed his eyes.

"Come. Here," he said. "Giddy. Up. Woe. Not 'woe' meaning sorrow and misfortune. But *w-h-o-a*, Blondie. Meaning 'stop.' And Blondie obeyed every one of those orders."

Bob walked over to his own bunk and sat down. He was frowning thoughtfully.

"You're onto something, Jupe," he said. "But when Pete called her, he used some of those same words and she didn't give him the time of day."

"I know," Jupe admitted, sounding as puzzled as Bob. "I realize it's impossible, but you'd think that little animal had met me before somewhere. She seemed to recognize my voice!"

5

Eavesdroppers

THAT NIGHT, AFTER A GOOD STEAK DINNER THAT Ascención barbecued for them, the Three Investigators went to sleep early.

Jupe was awakened a few hours later by a rubbing sound against the window beside his bunk. Raising his head, he saw that Blondie was outside. She was doing her best to push her nose in through the glass.

Jupe grumbled to himself and shook his fist at her, but she wouldn't go away. If Pete and Bob woke up and saw this, they'd never stop teasing him. Still mumbling, he got out of bed and walked to the door that led straight into the back yard. The moment he opened it, the burro stuck her head into the room. Jupe pushed hard against her chest, trying to keep her out. The little animal was as solid and unyielding as a sandbag. He couldn't move her. He finally slipped past her and, stepping outdoors, softly called her name.

She turned at once and trotted toward him. In the moonlight he could see that the hobbling rope was gone from her front legs. She was free. If he went back to his bunk, she would probably try to follow him.

You little pest, he thought. How am I going to get rid of you? The only answer seemed to be to lead her back to her own field. He started toward it, then suddenly stopped dead.

He could hear the sound of Spanish from the back porch at the far end of the house. A man's voice and then a woman's. Although Ascención never said a word to Dusty, he had been quite friendly to the three guys at the barbecue. Speaking Spanish to Jupe, he had asked them questions about the United States, talked about the lake, and warned them not to swim in it. He had told them the mountain water was ice cold and no one could last more than a few minutes in it. Jupe instantly recognized Ascención's gravelly voice now, but he was too far away to hear what the Mexican was saying.

Wondering who the woman was, Jupe moved closer to the back porch. Blondie walked beside him. Jupe stroked her neck to keep her from braying.

The woman was talking now. "You must help me, Ascención," Jupe heard her say in Spanish. "You know what Rice will do if he finds them. He might even kill them."

Ascención replied with several Mexican swear words describing the rancher. "All right. I'll do everything I can to help you," he promised. "You can count on me."

The woman thanked him. Jupe quickly withdrew

into the darkness as he heard her light footsteps coming down into the yard. He caught a glimpse of her before she vanished around the end of the building.

She had her back to him so he couldn't see her face. But the moonlight shone briefly on her blond hair.

The burro was rubbing her shoulder against Jupe. From where he was standing he could see that the gate into Blondie's field was open. He led her through it, closing and latching the gate after him. Then he climbed back into the yard. The burro hung her head over the fence, braying complainingly. Jupe was relieved to see she was no jumper. He want back to bed.

The next morning he had a quick word with the other two Investigators before they left their room. He told them what had happened during the night and explained that he had an important phone call to make. He wanted them to get Dusty away from the house for a couple of hours.

Ascención had made scrambled eggs with green peppers for breakfast. It was one of Jupe's favorite dishes and contained no starch, but he politely refused any. He said he had a slight stomach ache.

That was Pete's cue. He asked Dusty if he would take them fishing in the lake. The rancher agreed. Jupe announced he would stay at the ranch house because of his stomach. Half an hour later he was alone with Ascención.

A plate of fresh rolls had been left on the table. Jupe

fought a brief battle with himself. They smelled so good. Jupiter grabbed a few and stuffed them quickly into his mouth. After all, he had to have *something* to keep up his strength till lunchtime. He looked around for the phone.

He found it in Dusty's small office off the living room. Closing the door behind him, Jupe sat down at the desk and looked through the phone book for the direct-dial numbers to California.

Hector Sebastian answered at once. Jupiter told him where he was and came straight to the point.

"Could you do me a favor and call my computer information service from your terminal?" he asked his old friend.

Hector Sebastian was a successful mystery writer. He had once been a private eye himself and enjoyed giving the Three Investigators an assist with their cases whenever they asked him.

"No problem," the writer told him.

"Great," Jupe said. "All you need to do is enter my password. It's D-E-T-E-C-T. Then flip through the menus till you access the encyclopedia."

"Right," Hector Sebastian said. "And the subject is . . ."

"Uh, burros," the Investigator told him.

"Come again?"

"You know, burros, the small donkeys used as beasts of burden."

"Gotcha."

Jupe read off the questions about burros he needed

answered. Sebastian noted them down and promised to phone Jupiter as soon as he had the answers.

While he was waiting, Jupe looked around the small office. Ordinarily he would have thought twice before snooping on anyone. But he figured Dustin Rice had told the guys nothing but lies since he had first shown up at Jupe's house. The Three Investigators had a right to find out as many hard facts as they could.

Jupe's mind buzzed with questions. Why was *his* puzzle chosen out of the many perfect entries? Why was Rice so eager for him to get to the ranch fast? What made that Mexican woman want to stop him? And why did Blondie seem to know Jupe, though she'd never seen him before?

Jupe didn't come across anything of interest on Dusty's shelves except some large-scale maps of the Sierra Madre. Someone had penciled question marks all over them. Probably Dusty. In the top drawer of the desk were the deeds to the ranch. Jupe glanced through them until he came to the signature at the end.

ASCENCIÓN BARBERA.

So Ascención had sold the ranch to Dusty and become his field hand and cook. It seemed to explain the Mexican's hostility to the rancher.

In the bottom drawer of the desk was a tape recorder. Jupe took it out, turned down the volume, and pressed the play button.

This time he recognized his own voice at once.

He heard himself saying the same words again and again.

"Come. Here. Blondie. Giddy. Up. Woe. Blondie. Come. Here. . . ."

After a while, he carefully rewound the tape and put the recorder back where he had found it.

A few minutes later the phone rang. "I've got that info for you," Hector Sebastian told him. "Ready?"

"Yeah." Jupe turned over his list of questions and scribbled the answers on the back.

"Thanks," he said when the mystery writer had finished. "That's super."

"Any time, Jupe. Give me a call when you get back and I'll treat you troublemakers to a meal. I'm curious about where these burros are going to take you."

Jupe promised he'd call and thanked Sebastian again before he hung up. He had a lot to tell Pete and Bob and a pile of questions to chew over with them. But they wouldn't be back for at least an hour. He left the office, closing the door carefully behind him.

He hadn't seen Blondie that morning. Now that he had the answers to his questions about burros, he felt more interested in the little animal. He decided to pay her a visit.

Ascención was in the field with her, refilling her water tub. The moment the burro saw Jupe she trotted eagerly toward him. He patted her neck.

The Mexican had taken off his shirt in the noonday sun. Jupe noticed that his chest and back were the same even brown color as his face. Jupe couldn't tell if that was Ascención's own color or if a lot of work outdoors had deepened the man's naturally brown skin. For sure the Mexican was darker than Jupe. Even with daily swims, Jupe was still a pale Anglo who spent too much time indoors in front of his computer screen.

Jupe gestured at the burro. "Blondie's no longer . . ." He didn't know the Spanish word for "hobbled," but Ascención guessed what Jupe meant when he pointed to the burro's front legs.

"No, that ——" Ascención used the word that seemed to come naturally to him when he talked about Dusty. It was X-rated. "That —— took the rope off her yesterday evening."

"Why?"

"He's not afraid she'll run away now that you're here."

"Me? Why me?"

"She's grateful to you."

"What for?"

"She thinks you saved her life. And they are good animals, burros. Very faithful. Very grateful."

He picked up his bucket and walked away. Jupe went after him, followed by Blondie. But the Mexican refused to answer any more questions. He said he had work to do.

Pete and Bob had caught several trout. Ascención grilled them for lunch. Jupe suddenly recovered from his stomach ache and ate two of them. After all, they were pure protein.

"Let's walk off those calories," Jupe said after the meal. "How about it, guys?"

Pete and Bob guessed at once that he wanted to talk to them alone. The three of them set out across the fields to a clump of woods near the lake.

As soon as they were settled in a clearing among the trees, Jupe told them about his call to Hector Sebastian. He pulled his sheet of notes out of his jeans pocket.

"Burros have a very good sense of hearing," he reported. "Amazingly good. And they're not like dogs. They don't recognize people by their smell. Mostly by their voices. They'll often attach themselves to one person and when they do, they'll respond at once to that person's voice."

"You mean once they fall for you, they're hooked for life," Bob said. "Looks like Blondie's all yours."

"Knock it off," Jupe growled. "I bet that's what the whole moronic crossword contest was about. Dusty was looking for a voice that matched some other guy's. Some young American who had been a friend to Blondie."

He explained what Ascención had said.

"Somebody who saved her life at some time. I don't know how. And I don't know who that guy was. But when Dusty heard my entry to the competition, he thought my voice was closest to that other person's. So he edited my tape onto the machine I found in his desk this morning. He kept only the words he needed. Come here, Blondie, whoa, and so on. Then he tried those words out on the burro. But I guess the taped voice didn't work. Not very well, anyway. So Dusty couldn't be sure until we got here and Blondie could hear my natural voice. That's why he was so nervous all through breakfast yesterday. He couldn't wait to find out. And when it did work—remember how excited he got?"

Pete and Bob were silent for a moment, thinking over what Jupe had said.

"Makes sense so far," Bob agreed. "But . . ."

"Yeah," Pete put in. "But what's it all about? Why spend all that dough and waste all that time to find a voice a little Mexican burro thinks she recognizes?"

Jupe shook his head. "Beats me," he admitted. "But something else bugs me even more than that."

"What?" Bob asked.

"We know it's possible," Jupe explained, "to find two people whose voices sound alike. You thought that was my voice on the tape I found in my mailbox, Pete. But it's less than one chance in several billion that those two people also look alike."

He glanced at his page of notes. "And burros also have excellent eyesight," he went on. "In many ways better than we have. They don't recognize people *only* by their voices. They recognize them by sight as well."

Bob nodded. "Yeah, that does seem to—" His voice broke off.

The other two guys had heard it too. The sound of footsteps hurrying away, deeper into the woods. Moving as quietly as they could, the Three Investigators set off trying to follow the sound.

But the eavesdropper knew the woods better than they did. They soon lost the trail. They heard no more footsteps. Nothing but the flutter of birds.

They decided to split up and search the whole area separately.

Jupe was the first one back at the clearing. He hadn't found anyone. A few minutes later Pete joined him. He shook his head when Jupe glanced at him. Then the tall guy sprawled on the grass.

They had to wait another ten minutes for Bob. He had his hands in his pockets and was smiling in the cool, casual way that often meant he knew something the others didn't.

"You see someone?" Pete asked him. "Or is that classified info?"

"Not a living soul," Bob told him. He leaned against a tree. "But I did find this."

He took his right hand out of the pocket of his jeans. He was holding something between his fingers.

Jupe and Pete could see it was a piece of wool about three inches long. The kind of rough wool Mexicans made shawls out of.

The wool was bright purple.

6

A Sudden Hang-up

"I'M WORRIED ABOUT BLONDIE," DUSTY SAID AT BREAKfast the next morning.

Pete looked up from his ham and eggs. "What's wrong with her?" he asked. "Got her mind on something? Is she moody? Staring into space?"

Jupe kicked him under the table.

Dusty continued as if he hadn't heard. The rancher was in one of his nervous moods. He had eaten hardly any breakfast. "That burro will soon be in trouble if she stays in that field."

Jupe had seen the burro for a moment that morning. It seemed to him she was doing fine in her field. Grazing on the long grass, she looked healthy. Her coat was smooth, her eyes bright. She had been outside her shed when Jupe appeared and had galloped to meet him. She could gallop surprisingly fast.

He decided to keep all this to himself. Maybe Dusty would reveal another clue to the puzzle.

"Isn't Blondie getting enough to eat?" Jupe asked innocently.

"I'm worried about her hooves." The rancher frowned over his coffee. "You see, burros originally came from North Africa. They're used to hard, stony ground. Their hooves grow very fast, like toenails. Rocks and gravel keep them filed down. If burros stay too long in a soft, grassy place, their hooves keep growing until they double up under their feet." He put his coffee down. "After a while it cripples them."

"Can't you trim them?" Pete asked.

He'd once watched a friend do just that with a straight-edged razor.

"Nah." Dusty was still frowning. "A wild burro like that. She won't let me near her. She'd kick out at once if I even tried to touch her legs."

Jupe thought Blondie would probably let *him* trim her hooves. But he kept quiet. He could feel that Dusty was leading up to something. Something that had nothing to do with Blondie's toenails.

"I think I really ought to turn her loose," Dusty went on. "Let her go back into the mountains where she came from." He looked at Jupe. "The trouble is, she won't leave now. Now that you're here."

Jupe remembered what Ascención had said. "He's not afraid she'll run away now that you're here." Jupe could have asked Dusty why he hadn't turned Blondie loose weeks ago. He must have known about her hooves then. But he realized that the rancher was getting to the point now. The real point that would bring the Three Investigators one step closer to solving this case.

"Unless you went with her, Jupe," Dusty said thoughtfully. "I mean, we could all go. Take a little camping trip up into the mountains." He glanced at the three guys. "How does it sound to you?"

It sounded about as phony as a three-dollar bill to Jupe. He caught Bob's eye and gave him a quick wink.

Bob understood Jupe's signal at once. It meant, let's stall until we've talked about this. "We'll get back to you," Bob said.

"When?" Dusty asked anxiously. "How soon—"

"As soon as we've made up our minds," Pete explained, heading for the door, followed by his two friends. The three guys walked across the lower field until they were well out of hearing of the house.

"I guess it's almost time for the main event," Bob said when they were settled on the grass. "That trip into the mountains is what this riff's all about. That what you figure, Jupe?"

"Yeah." Jupe nodded. "That's what Dusty needed me for. My voice. So that Blondie wouldn't just run away. She'd *lead* us somewhere. Somewhere up in the mountains where she came from."

"What's way up there?" Pete wanted to know, glancing at the high range beyond the ranch. "Gold?"

"Sure." Bob smiled. "The treasure of the Sierra Madre." He picked a blade of grass and chewed it. "Well, how does it grab you guys? Want to hit the trail?"

"Okay with me," Pete decided. He enjoyed camping out, cooking over a wood fire, lying in a sleeping bag under the night sky. "How about you two? It might get pretty rough up there."

"No rougher than a road trip with a rock band," Bob said. "And that can be plenty rough." He looked at Jupe. "Whaddaya say?" he asked.

Jupe had never thought of himself as the outdoor type. He would rather think with his brains than his feet. But as an Investigator, he'd had to do a lot of hard legwork in the past. And they were going to solve this case no matter what it took.

"Sure," he said. "Sierra Madre, here we come. Let's go tell Rice the good news."

Jupe was right. It *was* good news to Dusty. He grinned broadly when Pete told him.

"What say we start tomorrow?" Dusty suggested eagerly.

The Three Investigators agreed that the next day would be fine. Still grinning, the rancher drove off to Lareto to buy supplies for the trip. Pete gave him a big stack of "Miss you" and "Wish you were here" greeting cards to mail to Kelly. Then the three guys split up until lunchtime.

Pete went down to the lake to fish. Bob settled on the porch to clean and disinfect his contact lenses. It was a chore he had to do every week and it might be difficult on the trip. Jupe went to look for Ascención. He had some questions he wanted to ask him.

He found the ranch hand in the kitchen trying to fix a walkie-talkie. He had taken it apart but didn't seem to be able to put it back together again.

"It's not my trade," the Mexican grumbled in Spanish. "Radios. What do I know about radios? Cattle, horses—that's what I know about."

"Let me try," Jupe offered. "I'm used to working with gadgets. Doesn't it work at all?"

"No. Of course not. Do you think I pulled it apart to amuse myself? I couldn't get a sound out of it."

"What do you use it for?"

"To talk into."

"Is there someone else around here who has one of these things?" Jupe was wondering whom Ascención found to talk to. Except for that distant church tower on the other side of the lake, he hadn't seen any buildings within miles of the ranch.

"Not as far as I know."

"Then why do you want it fixed?"

"Because it's broken."

Jupe had to be satisfied with that. He soon discovered what was wrong with the walkie-talkie's receiver—a faulty connection. He didn't have the right kind of wire to mend it with. So he had to improvise, stripping a length of electrical cord and using the thin copper wire from that.

"Have you known many young Americans?" he inquired in a casual, friendly way as he worked.

"No." The Mexican was watching him with grave interest. "Are they all as good at fixing things as you are?"

"Some of them." Jupe tried again. "Have there been any other young American guys staying at the ranch?"

"When?"

"In the past three or four months. Since Blondie came here."

Ascención shrugged. "Sometimes people stop by," he said.

"Did any of them sound like me? You know, my voice."

The Mexican's craggy face had its usual impassive look, but his dark eyes were smiling.

"All North Americans sound alike to me," he said.

"They don't all sound alike to Blondie."

"Burros have better ears than I do."

It was a no-go situation, Jupe realized. Ascención knew he was being pumped for information and he wasn't going to spill.

Jupe finished reassembling the device and switched it on. He couldn't get any response to his call signals, no matter how he adjusted the antenna, but he was satisfied the walkie-talkie was working again. If there was anyone with another walkie-talkie within range, Ascención would be able to communicate with them.

"There. It's okay now," he said.

"Very clever, you Americans."

"Thank you."

Maybe Americans were clever at some things. But Jupe knew he would have to get up very early in the morning to outsmart this Mexican.

Ascención picked up the walkie-talkie and thanked Jupe. Then he reached out and shook Jupe's hand.

"One day we'll have a long talk," he said. "One day

when—" He broke off. The phone was ringing. He went to the office to answer it. He was back almost at once.

"It's for you."

It must be Hector Sebastian, Jupe thought. He couldn't think of anyone else who could be calling him here.

But the mystery writer didn't answer when Jupe picked up the phone. A woman did. An American woman.

"Is this Jupiter Jones?" she asked.

"Yes. Who's this?"

"Never mind my name. It wouldn't mean anything to you anyway. I have something to show you. Something that's very important to you."

Jupe felt a quickening of interest, the excitement he always felt when a case took an unexpected turn.

"Why don't you come here to the ranch?" he suggested.

"No." A sudden note of fear crept into her voice. "I can't come to Dustin Rice's ranch. It would be much too dangerous for me."

"Dustin Rice isn't here," Jupe reassured her. "He's gone into Lareto."

"No." She still sounded scared. "Someone might see me and tell him. I want you to meet me on the other side of the lake."

She gave him detailed instructions. He would find a boat pulled up on the shore below the ranch. If he rowed across the lake and walked through the woods toward the church tower he would come to a small village. She would be waiting for him in the main square.

"Come alone," she finished. "If I see anyone with you, I'll leave. And you'll never find out what I have."

"What *do* you have?"

But there was only a humming sound on the line. She had hung up.

7

Jupe Takes the Bait

JUPE WALKED BACK ONTO THE PORCH. BOB HAD finished cleaning his contact lenses and was now reading his paperback history of Mexico. Jupe told him about the phone call.

"Something she wants to show you," Bob said. "Maybe she's got a picture of that American guy who was so tight with Blondie."

Jupe shrugged. He had thought the same thing himself. But he knew he was only guessing.

"Want me to come with you?" Bob asked.

Jupe told him the woman had insisted he row across alone.

"Hmmm," said Bob. "Well, you'll be right out in the open. I guess you can't get into any trouble. And all that exercise will do you good."

"Give me a break," Jupe groaned, heading for the lake.

Jupe couldn't see any sign of Pete when he reached the lakeshore. He soon found the solitary boat, a small wooden dinghy. Two oars were stowed under the seat.

54

He pushed the dinghy out onto the water, stepped in, and fitted the oars into the oarlocks.

He began to row.

He found it much more difficult than he'd expected. No matter how hard he pulled, the boat kept drifting sideways. He soon realized why. The lake was not a body of still water. A mountain river flowed into it at one end and out at the other. Even quite close to shore the current was stronger than the tide at Rocky Beach.

Jupe analyzed the problem for a moment, then turned the boat so that it was angled across the lake, into the current. By pulling harder on the right oar, the downstream oar, than on the left, he kept the boat moving toward the far shore without too much drift. But he had to put all his strength into it. Then—

CRACK!

The blade of his right oar broke off.

Jupe saw it float quickly away from him. He was left pulling a useless pole. He couldn't catch the water with it. He hurriedly jerked it into the boat and fitted the other oar into its place.

Now it was impossible to row the dinghy in a straight line. It kept spinning around like a dog chasing its own tail. Jupe tried switching the oar from side to side, but that was too slow and cumbersome. Finally he took the oar out of the oarlock and used it like a canoe paddle. Pulling desperately, first on one side and then on the other, he managed to force the boat unsteadily across the lake.

He was still less than halfway across when the second blade broke off.

Jupe was at the mercy of the current now. He tried poling the boat with one of the broken oars. The water was too deep. He couldn't reach the bottom.

He thought about shouting for help. But even if Bob or Ascencion heard him, what could they do without another boat?

He was powerless, drifting rapidly toward the river that surged out of the lake.

Jupe was a good swimmer. He could dive in and try to swim ashore against the current. But he remembered what Ascención had told them. Dipping his hand in, he found the Mexican had been right. The water was ice cold. He wouldn't last more than a few minutes in it.

At least he was still in the boat. If he stayed in the dinghy he would float on down the river. But for how long? The road up to the ranch had been a steep climb. The river back down would drop quickly. There would probably be rapids.

He thought of the village hidden on the other side of the lake. Maybe someone there had a boat.

"Help! Help me!" he yelled in Spanish. But the lakeside was deserted in the midday heat. A dog barked but no one responded.

Jupe tried to keep cool. To form a plan. Maybe he would find shallow places in the river. He might be able to pole himself to the bank.

He would soon find out. He wasn't far from the

mouth of the lake now. He could see where the water disappeared.

Disappeared!

Jupe knew what that meant—the top of a waterfall! He crouched in the boat, bracing himself for the shock, the sudden plunge over the edge.

"Jupe!"

He raised his head. Pete was standing on the bank of the lake, waving his fishing rod.

Pete didn't know about the broken oars. But he realized at once how much danger his friend was in. Unlike Jupe, he could see the thirty-foot drop where the lake narrowed and spilled into the river below. He had been fishing around the bottom of those falls. He had seen how powerful the rush of icy water was there. It would pound the wooden dinghy to pieces against the rocks below. And Jupiter . . .

Pete ran at full speed along the bank away from the falls. He stopped at the point where the land reached out farthest into the lake. He judged Jupe would have to pass within sixty feet of him before he was swept over the falls.

Pete released the catch on his reel and brought the rod back over his head. He had one chance. One only. There wouldn't be time for a second try. He braced himself, waiting until the dinghy was almost directly in front of him.

Using all the strength of his wrist and forearm, he whipped the rod forward and cast the lead sinker as far as he could across the lake.

It was the best and longest cast Pete had ever made. The sinker landed in the water just on the far side of the dinghy.

Jupe grabbed the line as it fell across the bow of the boat.

"Don't pull on it," Pete shouted to him. "It might snap. Hold on to the sinker."

Jupe pulled the lead weight out of the water and held it carefully with his right hand.

Pete began slowly and cautiously to reel in the line. Taking advantage of every inch of slack, he put as little strain on the nylon thread as possible.

He didn't try to pull the dinghy in toward the shore. But when the line was taut, he saw with a surge of relief that the boat began slowly circling in toward him as though held on a leash. He managed to reel in another few feet of slack.

As the dinghy came closer to the edge of the lake, the current grew weaker. Pete reeled in again, shortening the leash. The circle grew smaller. The boat was heading to shore. It was almost free of the current. Jupe was almost safe.

He was still ten yards from the bank when the line broke.

He kneeled on the seat and snatched up one of the broken oars. Leaning over the side, he plunged it as deep as he could into the water. Down, down it went. Then it suddenly struck bottom. He pushed on it, poling as hard as he could.

With terrible slowness the boat lurched a few feet

toward the bank. Jupe poled again. The dinghy heaved toward the shore once more. He was in less than a foot of water now. Jumping over the side, he grabbed the bow of the dinghy and waded the last few yards to the bank.

Pete ran to him and helped lift the boat ashore.

"Thanks," Jupe said. What else was there to say?

"Biggest fish I ever caught." Pete smiled. "I'll ask Ascención to grill you for lunch."

"I just don't want to be a frozen fillet."

They both heard the sound of quick footsteps as Bob came running around the edge of the lake. After Jupe had left him, he had wandered down to the shore to see how Jupe was making out. He had seen Jupe drifting toward the falls but there hadn't been a thing he could do to help him.

"Good casting," he told Pete. "Any Hollywood producer would be proud of a piece of casting like that."

Pete grinned. "Hey, I thought this was supposed to be *The Treasure of the Sierra Madre*, not *Jaws*! Besides, there's no way I'm going to be the one to tell Aunt Mathilda the bad news."

Jupe laughed with them. "Some pals!" He sat down and tugged off his wet sneakers and socks. After only a few seconds in the water, his feet were blue with cold. Lucky he hadn't tried to swim for it.

While Pete reeled in his line, Jupe quickly explained what had happened. The phone call. The broken oars.

"Both blades snapped off?" Pete asked. "Just like that?"

"No, not just like that." Jupe was looking at the smoothly broken ends of the oars. "They've been sawed through. So the blades would break off after a few minutes of rowing. Looks like someone was hoping I'd have a fatal accident."

He looked at Bob.

"Did you see anyone?" he asked. "Anyone on the other side of the lake?"

Bob nodded, sitting down on the stern of the boat. "Yeah, just for a second," he said. "I got a glimpse of a woman on the opposite shore. She seemed to be watching you, Jupe, as you were heading for the falls. Then she split."

"What did she look like?" Pete asked. "No, don't tell me. See if I can guess. A Mexican woman with long black pigtails and a purple shawl over her head."

Bob shook his head. "No, she looked like an American to me. She was wearing blue jeans and shades and—"

"And she had blond hair," Jupe interrupted him.

Bob looked startled. "Have you got ESP or something?"

8

Leave It to Blondie

THE NEXT MORNING THE THREE INVESTIGATORS SET off into the mountains.

Dusty had brought a horse box back with him from Lareto, hitched on to the back of the Jeep. Ascención caught one of the horses in the lower field. Pete helped him bridle and saddle it. The horse had been well broken in and made no trouble as Pete led it up the ramp into its new trailer home.

He stayed with it, brushing its coat, while Jupe and Ascención went to get Blondie. Jupe was glad to have a little time alone with Ascención. He wanted to try to get some more information out of the wary Mexican.

"That boat down there on the edge of the lake," he asked, "is it always kept there?"

"Where else would you keep a boat? In the kitchen?"

"Who does it belong to?"

"The ranch."

"Does anyone ever use it?"

"Sometimes."

"What for?"

"Fishing."

As usual in his attempts to pry information out of Ascención, Jupe wasn't getting very far. But there was still one thing he had to know.

The blond woman Bob had seen across the lake was almost certainly the American woman who had phoned Jupe. So she was probably also the one who had sawed through the oars. But how had she made the journey back and forth across the water? She would have had to do that early the previous morning or maybe during the night.

"If you wanted to get to that village on the other side of the lake," he asked Ascención, "how would you do it?"

"Walk."

"But the lake's very deep."

"It isn't deep up there." The Mexican pointed toward the river that flowed into the upper end of the lake. "There are stepping stones."

Jupe nodded. That seemed like a possible answer. The American woman had crossed to Dusty's ranch on the stepping stones, tampered with the oars, then crossed back to phone Jupe from the village.

And if she was the same blond woman Jupe had glimpsed that first night in the moonlight, then Ascención knew her.

"Do you have any friends in the village?" Jupe asked.

"I know the man who owns the bar, the cantina. He's my cousin."

"Any American friends? A woman with blond hair?"

They had reached the gate into Blondie's field. Ascención turned and faced Jupe. He looked the American in the eye.

"It was stupid what she did," he said suddenly, his tongue loosened. "I told her it was stupid. But she's very frightened. And when people are frightened, they sometimes do senseless things. I'm glad you weren't hurt. But . . ."

He touched Jupe's shoulder.

"Be careful in the mountains, amigo," he warned him. "It's dangerous in the mountains."

Blondie was galloping excitedly to meet Jupe. He opened the gate and she rubbed her muzzle against him. Jupiter scratched her behind the ears. Blondie was growing on him. She still wouldn't let Ascención touch her. The Mexican had to stand at a distance while he told Jupe how to bridle her with a rope.

"You'll have to ride her without a saddle," he explained. "No matter how much she likes you, she won't put up with being saddled. She'll roll over and over on the ground until she tears the cinch loose."

Jupe's eyes widened.

Dusty had loaded the back seat of the Jeep with their supplies. Sacks of beans and rice, oats for the horse, sugar and coffee, sleeping bags, a rifle. Pete and Bob had to squeeze in back among all the provisions. Jupe sat in front with the rancher, holding Blondie on a long lead. She trotted beside the Jeep and the horse box trailed behind it.

He looked back as they drove through the gate at the bottom of the field. Ascención was standing on the porch. He raised his right hand just before Jupe lost sight of him.

It wasn't so much a good-bye as a gesture of warning.

Winding up into the hills, Dusty had to drive very slowly, keeping his speed down to five or six miles an hour, so that Blondie could keep up with the Jeep without tiring herself. For the first hour they were on a dusty road littered with stones. Then that petered out into little more than a track threading between the pine trees.

After another hour, Dusty pulled to a stop to let the engine cool. When the rancher turned off the motor, Jupe could hear the sound of running water. Blondie was tugging at the rope.

"I guess she's thirsty," he told Dusty. "Probably hungry, too. I'd better go with her so she won't try to run off."

Jupe let the little burro lead him to the edge of a mountain stream. The water looked clear and inviting. Jupe realized he was thirsty too. Ascención had told him it was okay to drink from running streams in the Sierra Madre, although not from any lakes or ponds. He kneeled down and drank from his cupped hands. Blondie lowered her head and drank beside him.

When she had had enough to drink, the burro began to graze. They hadn't brought along any supplies for her on the trip. Unlike the horse, Blondie could look out for herself. Ascención had told them burros were great foragers. "As good as goats," the Mexican had said.

After Blondie had grazed for several minutes, Jupe heard Dusty calling impatiently from the Jeep. Jupe tried to lead the burro back to it. No matter how hard he pulled on the rope, saying, "Come on. Come on, you stubborn little animal," she wouldn't move. He had to wait until she had eaten her fill of grass.

Dusty was gunning the engine furiously when Jupe and Blondie got back. The others had all finished the lunch Ascención had packed for them. Jupe managed to gulp down his sandwich with one hand as the Jeep bounced over the ruts. He still held Blondie's lead with the other hand. Dusty drove another three hours, until even the dirt track disappeared.

"We'll have to leave the Jeep here," he said.

They unloaded the supplies. Pete led the horse out of its box. Dusty drove both vehicles under some trees and they covered them with pine branches. Then the rancher packed the heavier bundles onto the horse, and Blondie let Jupe fasten the sleeping bags across her shoulders.

"You lead the way," Dusty told Jupe when they were ready to go. "Just let the burro have her head and pick the trail."

Jupe exchanged glances with his friends.

They set off again. Jupe sat astride Blondie, bareback. Pete and Bob, carrying only their own backpacks, followed him on foot. Dusty came last, riding the heavily loaded horse with the rifle in his saddle holster.

Jupe found it was a full-time job keeping his seat on the burro. He couldn't let his mind wander for a second. They were soon above the tree line, climbing gullies so steep and rocky that Pete and Bob had to scramble up them on all fours. Blondie took them in her stride. Ascención had said she could live off the land like a goat. She could climb like a goat, too. Jupe had to keep his arms around her neck so he wouldn't slide off over her rump.

At least he was having an easier time of it than Dusty. Compared to the burro, the horse was clumsy and halting. The rancher often had to dismount and tug the unwilling animal over the rocks by her bridle. He was losing ground and was soon a quarter of a mile behind Pete and Bob.

Jupe decided to stop for a while to give the others a chance to catch up.

"Whoa," he shouted into Blondie's ear. "W-h-o-a!"

But the burro had no intention of stopping. She was enjoying her climb and wasn't going to wait for anybody. Jupe was getting annoyed with her stubbornness. He tugged on her bridle to show her who was boss. She didn't pay any attention to that either.

Then suddenly she stopped dead.

She did it so unexpectedly that Jupe almost pitched forward over her ears. They had reached a ledge of level ground. Weeds were growing up through the stones. A clump of cactus stood directly in front of them.

Jupe guessed Blondie probably wanted to graze again. He relaxed and dismounted. This seemed a good place for him to take a rest too. He could see a flat rock beside the cactus. He started toward it.

Blondie instantly stretched out her neck, blocking his way. When he tried to slip past her, she grabbed the loose hem of his T-shirt between her teeth and jerked him back.

"Okay, what do you want now?" Jupe asked angrily. "If you want to graze, go ahead. But don't graze on my T-shirt." He tried to pull it loose from her teeth. She held on.

Jupe finally shrugged and gave in. There was no arguing with the burro when she had made up her mind about something. At the moment she had obviously decided to remain exactly where she was. And she wanted Jupe to stay there with her.

When he patted her side, she did let go of his T-shirt. But she didn't move out of his way. She swung her neck back and looked straight at the cactus.

And then Jupe noticed her ears.

They were laid straight back along her neck.

And the silky hairs on her neck were no longer lying flat against her skin.

They were bristling with fear.

9

Who's the Boss?

JUPE STOOD PERFECTLY STILL, WATCHING THE cactus.

Pete and Bob scrambled up beside him. "What gives?" Pete asked.

"I don't know. Something scared Blondie."

Bob started forward. Pete held him back. He had also noticed the bristling hairs on the burro's neck. "See what she does next," he said.

Blondie did nothing, still staring rigidly at the cactus. For a minute all they could hear was the rancher's horse panting as it labored up the trail and came to a halt behind them.

"What's holding you guys up?" Dusty snapped.

Then they heard it.

The faint buzzing that Blondie's sharp ears had caught much earlier. A sound that meant danger.

The buzzing came from some rocks behind the cactus. It wasn't as regular as the sound a bee makes. It broke off and then started again, louder, faster.

Standing beside his horse, Dusty drew in his breath

sharply. He reached for the rifle in his saddle holster.

"It's a rattler," he said. "It's waiting somewhere behind that cactus. Blondie must have set it off. We'll have to scare it out so I can get a shot at it."

The Three Investigators stooped and picked up stones. They held them ready to throw while the rancher leveled and aimed his gun.

"Now," Pete said.

All three guys threw their stones at the same moment. The buzzing stopped. But it wasn't followed by silence.

With a high-revved rattling sound the snake came slithering out from beneath the cactus. It was about four feet long. Its broad head raised, it moved frighteningly fast, coiling and uncoiling as it advanced.

The three guys took a quick step backward.

Dusty fired his rifle.

Pete couldn't tell if the rancher had hit the rattlesnake or not. He sure hadn't killed it. It darted to one side and kept coming.

Bob watched it with helpless fascination. It was heading straight for him now. He could see its flat eyes, its long darting tongue, the horny cluster of rattles at the end of its raised tail. He tried to move but he couldn't. He felt as though the snake had hypnotized him.

Dusty worked the bolt of his rifle and raised the barrel.

But he didn't squeeze the trigger. Blondie was directly in the line of fire.

The little burro's ears were laid flat back. She turned around rapidly until she was facing away from the snake.

Bob saw the rattler's head rise even higher. It poised itself for an instant, ready to strike.

Blondie kicked out savagely with both her hind legs.

The burro's hooves caught the rattler square across the thickest part of its raised body. It sailed up into the air and over the side of the ledge, falling onto the rocks twenty feet below. It lay there for a second as though stunned. Then it slithered out of sight.

Dusty slid his rifle back into his saddle holster.

No one spoke. They all stood there, taking deep breaths. Then without a word they set off on their way again.

Blondie had stopped climbing. She began to circle around the mountain until Jupe could see trees just below them again. The burro descended rapidly toward the trees. Although it seemed to Jupe she was doubling back on her own trail, he didn't try to restrain her. As Blondie entered the trees and came to a stop, he leaned forward and stroked her neck.

"Okay," he told her. "Whatever you say goes. From now on you're the boss."

When Dusty caught up with the three guys, he had to admit the burro had picked a good place to camp for the night. Firewood and grass were plentiful, and as Blondie showed Jupe by leading him to it, a spring of clear water flowed nearby.

It got cold when the sun went down. The Three

Investigators pulled on sweaters over their T-shirts. Pete soon had a good fire going and helped Dusty unload the horse. Dusty unsaddled, fed, and watered her. Then he cooked up a big pot of beans and rice.

Jupe looked at the food on his plate. Carbohydrates! He gulped. Beans weren't too bad. At least they contained protein as well as starch. But rice was pure poison. Nothing *but* starch.

Jupe came to a decision. He was on the trail of an exciting case. He needed his strength. Keil Halfebrot would have to take care of his own lettuce leaves for a while. Jupe plunged in and cleaned his plate.

And didn't ask for seconds. Somehow his stomach felt full. I must be too tired to eat, he thought.

After dinner Bob took off his sneakers and rubbed his feet. They were sore from all that climbing.

"How much farther are we going?" he asked the rancher.

Dusty looked at him sharply. "Aren't you enjoying the trip?"

Bob looked back at him even more sharply. "I was just thinking about Blondie's toenails," he said sarcastically. "Plenty of rocks and stones up here." He was fed up with Dusty's lies. And he wanted the impatient rancher to know that he and Jupe and Pete weren't just kids who would go along with anything Dusty cared to tell them. They hadn't fallen for that fairy tale about Blondie's toenails.

"Yeah," Pete chimed in. "Some of those trails were

rougher than a nail file. Why don't we turn her loose right here?"

Dusty didn't answer at once. He threw some sticks onto the fire. "That burro knows where she's going," he said at last. "She's heading back where she came from. And she'll know when she gets there."

"Home, sweet home," Jupe said thoughtfully. "Why do you think she ever cut out if the place meant so much to her?"

"It's hard to say," the rancher told him impatiently. "Sometimes wild burros just stray away from the herd. Who knows why?"

Jupe knew Dusty was lying again. Blondie hadn't just strayed all those miles down to the ranch. Someone had led her there. Someone she trusted and would follow. Maybe someone Blondie thought had saved her life, as Ascención had put it. Someone whose voice was uncannily like Jupe's.

The burro was grazing farther and farther from the fire. The rancher glanced uneasily at her. "You'd better tether her for the night," he warned Jupe. He managed a fake smile. "We don't want her wandering back to the ranch again."

Jupe hoisted himself to his feet. He had hardly noticed it while he was riding, but his legs were now so stiff he could hardly stand up. He walked over to Blondie like a man on stilts and gave her a pat on the rump. "You'll stick with *me*, right Blondie?" he said.

"Just the same, I'd feel safer if you tied her up," Dusty grumbled. "Go on, tether her to a tree."

Jupe turned and faced him. He shook his head.

"No," he said. "She might want a drink of water in the night."

"She's already had all the water she needs."

It was a showdown. Jupe knew it and he wasn't going to give in.

"You want her tied up, do it yourself," he said. "If she'll let you touch her."

His eyes met the rancher's for a long moment. Blondie might be the boss on the trail. But Jupe was the boss here now.

"Okay," Dusty agreed at last, crawling into his sleeping bag. "I guess she'll stick around as long as you're here."

"Why?" Jupe asked curtly. "Why do you think she's so attached to me?"

"*Quién sabe*, as the Mexicans say." The rancher turned over on his side and closed his eyes. "Who knows?"

Jupe hobbled back to the fire. Bob winked at him as he passed.

Jupe eased himself into his sleeping bag. Soon all four of them were asleep.

It was still dark when Jupe woke up. The fire had gone out and for a moment he was too sleepy to understand what had wakened him. Then he heard it again.

A protesting braying.

Blondie.

He scrambled stiffly out of his sleeping bag and felt his way between the trees to the spring.

As he entered the clearing he saw a streak of light. It moved up and down and around in circles. At first all he could see in the waving light beam was Blondie. She had reared up on her hind legs and was plunging wildly.

Then the light stilled for a moment and he saw the figure of a woman. She was holding a flashlight in one hand and tugging on the burro's rope with the other, trying to drag Blondie away into the trees.

Blondie brayed again. She reared still higher, ready to stamp on this stranger who was pulling at the rope around her neck.

Jupe knew how the burro dealt with rattlesnakes. He was more scared for the woman than he was for Blondie.

"Let her go," he shouted.

Running forward, he tried to calm the little burro. "Blondie. Steady, Blondie," he called in a soothing voice. Instantly the woman dropped the rope. Released, Blondie settled back on four legs. She turned to Jupe. He stroked her nose, looking at the woman.

The flashlight went out.

In the sudden darkness Jupe heard the sound of running. The woman had plunged away into the night. The next moment Pete and Bob joined Jupe in the clearing.

"What's going on?" Bob asked. "Blondie woke me up."

"Someone just tried to steal her," Jupe explained. "A woman . . ."

"Uh-oh," Pete said. "That blonde again. The one who tried to drown you. Is she after burros now?"

"No." Jupe shook his head. "I only saw her for a second in the flashlight. But I'd know her anywhere. She was that Mexican woman from the bus. The one with the purple shawl and the long black pigtails."

10

Stranger in the Night

THE NEXT TWO DAYS WERE LIKE THE FIRST. HOUR BY hour, mile by mile, they traveled deeper into the Sierra Madre. The mountains seemed to go on forever. As soon as they climbed to the top of one rise, they would see another one ahead.

Narrow valleys separated the ranges. For a few miles the Three Investigators would be surrounded by pine trees. Then, as they climbed again above the tree line, they would have to clamber up bare rocky gulleys until they were over another range.

"Lucky for us it's summer," Pete said as he and Bob scrambled over the rocks. "In winter we'd be up to our necks in snow."

"Doesn't sound that bad to me," Bob grunted. He was dripping with sweat.

Their day began as soon as the sun rose. They ate hot beans and rice for breakfast, cold beans and rice for lunch, hot beans and rice for dinner. It was boring and it was starchy but Jupe's guilt meter was on low. He was determined to solve this case and see where

Blondie was leading them. Everything else—even watching carbohydrates—was on hold. Anyway, he never wanted more than one serving of Dusty's glop.

Three or four times a day Blondie would stop to graze. The Three Investigators welcomed these halts. It gave them a chance to stretch out and rest. It also gave Dusty and his horse a chance to catch up. Although the rancher fed his horse plenty of oats, she seemed to get more tired each day. Sometimes she lagged a mile behind Pete and Bob.

At one of these rest stops, the Three Investigators lounged in the grass while Blondie munched.

"I want to know why these women have it in for us," Bob said. "First a blonde tries to deep-six Jupiter and then a brunette tries to steal our burro."

"Maybe the Mexican woman's burro went lame," Pete guessed, "and she needed something to carry her stuff."

Bob didn't buy it. "You'd think a Mexican would be sharper about burros. She'd know that you can't drag one off against its will."

"I wonder," said Jupe, "if she really wanted the burro for herself. My hunch is she just didn't want *us* to have her."

"Huh?" Pete said.

But Jupe had no more to say. The guys moved on.

Every evening before sunset Blondie found a place with water and firewood where they could camp for the night. They never saw another human being. Now and then they did see adobe huts with thatched roofs in the distance. But if anyone lived in them, they never showed themselves.

After the second day, Jupe's legs lost their stiffness. They developed muscles he never knew he had. On the third morning he made a wonderful discovery. His leather belt was too loose for him! He had to take it in a notch.

"It must be all this exercise, riding Blondie," he told his friends proudly.

That made Pete laugh. "No wonder you're losing weight," he said. "No chance for pigging out between meals."

Jupe didn't care about the teasing. Whatever the cause, he *was* thinner. And maybe he had a hope for a date before summer vacation was over. He started to whistle.

That day as they were moving along a ridge the three guys saw a plume of white smoke billow up from beyond a range of mountains ahead. They stopped and watched it.

"That's all we need," Bob said. "A forest fire."

"It's a long way off," Pete reassured him. "And maybe if we're lucky, the wind'll blow it the other way."

Jupiter looked thoughtful as they continued on.

That night Dusty arrived in camp an hour after the Three Investigators. He looked worried as he ate.

"I'm going to have to give the horse a day's rest before it goes lame," he said when he had finished his meal. "You push on without me. I'll catch up with you as soon as I can."

"Sure you can find us?" Pete asked.

"Don't worry about that. It'll be easy enough to track you in this kind of country. Two guys on foot and one riding a burro leave a pretty clear trail."

The next morning after Dusty had divided up the supplies, the Three Investigators set off on their own. Blondie didn't seem to mind being loaded with the food and the cooking pot as well as their sleeping bags. Jupe joined his friends on foot. They kidded and laughed as they camped that night, relieved to be away from Dusty.

"Let me guess what we're having," Bob said to Pete as Jupe made dinner. "Rice and beans?"

"Wrong!" Pete answered. "It's beans and rice."

"Actually," Jupe intoned nasally, "beans à la rice is the selection for this evening. Please prepare your dining utensils."

After dinner they were sitting around the fire when Blondie suddenly brayed with excitement. They all jumped to their feet, listening.

As usual, they didn't hear anything until long after Blondie had. Then they caught the sound of footsteps approaching out of the darkness.

A moment later the campfire lit up a large burro slowly ambling toward them. It was obviously much older than Blondie. It wasn't saddled, but there were several packs roped across its back.

The woman with the black pigtails was walking behind it.

Blondie stopped braying. She seemed delighted to see another of her own kind. She trotted forward and the two animals rubbed noses.

The Mexican woman came closer.

"Don't worry," she said in Spanish. "I haven't come to try to steal your burro this time. I want to talk to you. My name is Mercedes and I know who you all are. But before we talk, please give me something to eat. I'm hungry."

Jupe gave her a plate of rice and beans. Mercedes sat down by the fire. She obviously was hungry. She didn't say another word until she had finished.

Jupe had seen her only at a distance on the bus. This was his first chance to study her. He watched her guardedly while she ate.

She was around forty, he guessed. A good-looking woman with a strong, determined face. She was wearing a loose woolen skirt with pockets, Mexican boots, and a blouse with short sleeves. Her skin was deep brown and her eyes were as dark as Ascención's. On the whole, he guessed, she would make a good friend and a dangerous enemy.

She put aside her empty plate and glanced at the man's watch she was wearing. The strap had come loose and the watch had slid down her wrist. She quickly pushed it back into place.

"I don't have much time," she said, still in Spanish. "I've got to get back to the lake. So I'll tell you what I have to say as briefly as I can." She looked at Jupe. "I'm sorry I don't speak any English. But from what I saw of you on the bus trip, you understand Spanish quite well. No?"

Jupe remembered the Mexican guy in the torn leather jacket who had tried to stop them from getting back on the bus. She had obviously overheard Jupe's argument with him. And Jupe had seen her pay that man right afterward.

He nodded. "I can understand what you say," he told Mercedes. "If you speak slowly."

"Good." Mercedes drew her feet up, covering them with her skirt. Then for the next fifteen minutes she talked in a low, urgent voice. Jupe had to interrupt only now and then to ask her what a word meant. When she had finished, he felt confident he had understood her whole story.

Mercedes stood up. The Three Investigators got up too. She shook hands with each of them. Then, as suddenly and mysteriously as she had arrived, she led her burro off into the night.

Pete put more wood on the fire. "Okay, what was that all about?" he asked.

"What a story!" Jupe told his friends as they sprawled on the ground. "I'll run it by you in a minute. But first, Bob, give me the lowdown on Pancho Villa."

"What do I look like, the Mexican Public Library?" Bob exclaimed.

"Come off it. You've been reading that Mexican history book ever since we left Rocky Beach. Did you finish it yet?"

"Yeah." Bob smiled. "I finished it that day you almost became a historical item yourself by drowning in the lake."

"Great." Jupe smiled too. "The part I'm interested in is around 1916. What do you know about Pancho Villa?"

"There was a big revolution going on in Mexico then. Pancho Villa was one of the stars. Some people think he was just an outlaw, like Jesse James. But he managed his own private army. And he won a lot of battles."

"Did he spend any time up here in the Sierra Madre?"

"Yeah. This was one of his bases. He'd go swinging down into the desert and hold up trains. Then he'd hide out up here."

Jupe nodded thoughtfully. "At least Mercedes was telling the truth about that," he said.

"You mean that's what she was yakking about the whole time?" Pete asked. "About a dead guy called Pancho Villa?"

"No, not the whole time." Jupe looked at Bob and went on. "But we might be on the trail of that treasure of the Sierra Madre you're always going on about. Pancho Villa's loot. Mercedes said he robbed a train one day and got away with thousands and thousands of dollars' worth of silver pesos. Then he came up here and hid the money in a cave. Unluckily for him, he used the same cave to store his gunpowder in. One of his men got careless and the gunpowder exploded. Part of the mountain collapsed. It buried all those silver pesos under tons of rock and totaled some of Villa's soldiers. He started to clear away the fallen rock. But then the other side in the revolution attacked him and he had to get out of these mountains fast."

Jupe paused for a moment.

"Mercedes says the silver's still there," he finished.

Pete and Bob were silent while they thought that over.

"How did she get onto all this?" Pete wanted to know.

"She said her grandfather was one of Villa's soldiers and he passed the story down through the family."

"What was she saying about Dusty?" Bob asked. "I did catch *his* name. I made out something about a burro, too."

"I'm getting to that," Jupe told him. "She said about three months ago a close friend of hers, a young American named Brit, came out of these mountains. He and his father had been prospecting up here. Looking for Pancho Villa's cave. And they thought they'd found it. At least Brit told Mercedes they had."

Jupe paused again, remembering.

"Go on. Don't stop in the middle of a solo," Bob complained. "We're waiting for the part about Dusty and Blondie."

"When Brit got to the lake," Jupe went on, "he had a little white burro with him. He had found her running wild near the cave. He made friends with her and led her down to Dusty's ranch. Then he disappeared back into the mountains alone."

"Why?" Pete asked. "Why didn't he just leave her where she was?"

"Because Brit was afraid Blondie would die if she stayed in the mountains. He had to get a vet for her and the nearest one was in Lareto. Ascención did get the vet, who cured Blondie."

"What was wrong with her?" Pete demanded. "I mean, she couldn't have been all that sick if she made it as far as Dusty's ranch."

"She had a very bad eye infection." That was one of the parts of Mercedes' story that had most interested Jupe. It explained something that had been nagging at him for days. Why had Blondie recognized him *only* by his voice? Why didn't she know Jupe didn't *look* like the other young American, Brit?

"When Brit found her in the mountains," he continued, "Blondie was blind." Jupe remembered Ascención's words: She thinks you saved her life.

Pete whistled softly. "It does all begin to add up," he said. "If Dusty knew Brit and his father had found old Pancho Villa's silver—"

"Yeah," Jupe interrupted. "Mercedes says he tried to follow Brit back to it. But Brit was too fast and too smart for him. He covered his own tracks. So Dusty was left with Blondie. The only one who could lead him to the loot. But Blondie didn't want to lead him anywhere. Not without someone whose voice she thought she recognized."

"So Dusty had to find a voice that matched Brit's," Pete said. "That's what that whole puzzle contest was about."

"And you got the part, Jupe," Bob put in. "But what beats me is why Mercedes told you about the cave and those silver pesos."

"Yeah," Pete added. "Since she tried to keep us off the bus."

That same question had bothered Jupiter.

"She wouldn't let me ask her any questions," he said. "Except when I didn't follow her Spanish. So I'm just telling you what she told me. She doesn't trust Dusty farther than she can throw him. She doesn't believe his horse was going lame. She thinks he's only a few hours behind us. She's scared he'll kill Brit and his father when he finds them. And he'll kill *her*, too, if he sees her. So she said she was going back to the lake. And she wants us to get moving. Get to the cave and warn Brit and his father that Dusty is close behind us and may show up any minute."

There was a long silence while the Three Investigators gazed into the fire.

Pete finally spoke. "You believe her?" he asked Jupe.

"I don't know," Jupe admitted. "Why's she so hot on us finding Brit and his father? Or maybe it's the silver she wants us to find."

"Yeah," Bob agreed. "So she can follow us and get her hands on that dough herself."

11

Double Talk

THE NEXT MORNING THE THREE INVESTIGATORS WERE up before dawn. Over a quick breakfast they talked some more about Mercedes.

"She tried to con us at least once last night," Jupe remembered.

"How?" Pete asked.

"When she looked at her watch and said she had to get back to the lake. She wanted us to think she was leaving right away."

"You're right," Bob agreed. "Like, how far could she make it in these hills at night?"

"Something else about that watch," Jupe went on. "It had slipped down her wrist and when she pushed it back up, I thought"—he shrugged—"I don't know. Maybe it was just a trick of the firelight. I thought I saw a kind of scar on her wrist."

Neither of the others had noticed that. But Bob did have something else to add about Mercedes.

"She's one tricky lady, all right," he said with a grin. "For one thing, there aren't all that many

Mexican women who wear contact lenses. For another thing—"

"Contact lenses?" Pete interrupted.

"I saw her cleaning them on the bus. She kept her head down so I wouldn't see what she was doing. But she's got a little kit just like mine."

"What's the other thing?" Jupe demanded. He felt like blowing his top when Bob casually came out with delayed bits of information like that.

"The other thing"—Bob was still smiling maddeningly—"is what's she doing wandering around the Sierra Madre with a walkie-talkie?" He finished his beans and scraped his plate clean with a handful of pine needles while Jupiter silently counted to ten. "I thought I saw an antenna sticking out of one of those packs on her burro while she was giving you that pitch about Pancho Villa. So I checked it out. I'm telling you straight, she's got a walkie-talkie, all right."

"Who's she hoping to walkie-talk to way up here?" Pete wondered. "It can't be Dusty. I've helped him pack and unpack that dumb horse so many times, I can swear he hasn't got one."

"Ascención does," Jupe remembered. "I helped him fix it. But there's no way any walkie-talkie in the world could transmit from here all the way back to the ranch."

They stood up and carefully stamped out the fire. Then they packed up their gear and Jupe roped it onto Blondie's shoulders.

"What if," Jupe said thoughtfully, stroking the little

burro's neck, "what if Mercedes isn't going back to the lake. What if she's hiding out among the rocks right now." He looked around him in the gathering light. "Waiting for us to move on so she can follow our tracks. But she doesn't want us to catch on to the fact that she's after those pesos too."

Pete shrugged. "If that's what she wants, she's got us. There's no way we can hide all our tracks."

"True." Jupe started to lead the burro out of the clearing. "But we do have one advantage."

"What?"

"Blondie made friends with Mercedes' burro last night. And from what Hector Sebastian told me, once burros know each other, they can sense one another a long way off. And they'll bray to each other. So if Mercedes and her burro come within a couple of miles of us, Blondie will let us know it."

That day's journey was the hardest of all. Blondie had started climbing the tallest and steepest mountain they had seen. The little burro had to keep zigzagging along deep gullies as she moved slowly up toward the distant peak.

She never stopped or brayed. And though the Three Investigators kept glancing back, they never caught sight of Mercedes or her burro.

They did see another thick plume of smoke. It seemed to rise from around the flattened top of the mountain they were climbing.

"Weirdest forest fire I ever saw," Pete said. "Where's the forest? Not a thing up there except a few cactus."

"You're right," Jupe agreed. "But the smoke could be coming from the other side of the mountain. If the fire circles below us, we're going to get cut off."

"Great," Bob said. "Not only do we have a psychopathic liar and a shifty woman following us, but now we've got a forest fire to contend with too."

Pete was watching the sky. "Weirdest smoke I ever saw, too," he went on. "It goes up. But it doesn't stay there. It just disappears."

Bob looked up as flights of birds passed high overhead. Hawks and kites and vultures. "Lucky bums," he said. "Hightailing it out of here before they get cooked."

They pushed on. Jupe's eagerness to solve the riddle and his slimmer girth made it easy for him to bound up the trail after Blondie. By early afternoon he and the burro were well ahead of Pete and Bob.

Then the two guys suddenly heard Jupe's voice echoing down the mountainside.

"Stop," he yelled to them. "Stay where you are."

They both stopped at once. Looking up, they saw Jupe raise his hands above his head.

"Now come closer," they heard him call. "Just follow the burro slowly."

Bob and Pete looked at each other. What in the blue moon was Jupe talking about? Isn't that exactly what they'd been doing all this time—following Blondie?

Keeping their eyes on him, they started to crawl upward again. Jupe was walking close behind Blondie.

And for some reason they couldn't understand, he still had his hands raised.

Then he came to a dead stop.

"Don't come any closer," his voice echoed down to them. "Who are you? What are you doing here? What do you want?"

Pete and Bob looked at each other again. The whole situation was becoming more and more bizarre. It became just plain crazy a moment later when they heard Jupe's voice again.

"I'm Jupiter Jones," he called. "And I've got a message for you."

Jupe wasn't thinking of the effect his words were having on his friends. To him the situation wasn't weird—it was scary. He had come around a bend in the trail to see the barrel of a rifle sticking out of the rocks ahead of him.

"Stop," a voice had called to him. "Stay where you are."

What surprised Jupe the most was that at those words Blondie stood stock still. Her ears rose. She brayed softly.

Jupe obeyed the next order to follow Blondie slowly. The burro stopped a yard from the muzzle of the rifle. It was still pointing straight at Jupiter.

A guy about Jupe's age stepped out from the rocks.

He was taller than Jupe, with untidy blond hair and a deeply tanned face. He was wearing jeans and Mexican boots and a denim jacket. Even after Jupe had told him his name, the stranger kept the rifle leveled as he walked forward. But he was no longer looking at Jupe. He was staring at the little white burro.

"Blondie," he said. "How did you get here?" Blondie's ears quivered. She turned her head and glanced at Jupe. Then back at the guy with blond hair. She seemed totally confused.

Jupe patted her neck.

"I brought her," he said. "Or rather she brought me. Are you Brit?"

The blond guy didn't answer. Still aiming his rifle at Jupe, he stepped to the edge of the narrow trail and looked down the mountain. About thirty yards below, Pete and Bob were climbing slowly toward him.

"Who are those two *hombres*?" he asked suspiciously.

Jupe hastily explained they were friends of his from California.

"We came to help you, Brit," he went on. "You *are* Brit, aren't you?"

"Yeah." He didn't lower his rifle. "Help me? How?"

"By warning you that Dustin Rice—"

"Where is he?" There was a sudden wariness in Brit's eyes. "Is he down there with your friends?"

"No. He started out with us. But his horse started going lame. Or that's what he said. We left him miles back. But he could get here tomorrow."

"Thanks. Thanks for telling me." Brit slipped on the safety catch and slung the rifle across his shoulder. "How did you get up here?"

"Blondie brought us. She led us back where she came from."

"How did Dusty manage to tame her so fast?"

"He didn't. She's still pretty wild. I'm the only person she'll let near her. That's because she thinks I saved her life. She thinks I'm you."

"Me? Why?"

"Because of our voices. Maybe you haven't noticed, but our voices are really alike. To Blondie we must sound exactly the same. She thought she recognized my voice the first time she heard it. To her it was the voice that had guided her to safety when she was blind. She's come to associate that voice with the way I *look* now. That's why she's so puzzled by you."

Brit smiled at the burro. "Come here, Blondie," he said. "Good little Blondie, come here."

Blondie's ears were still quivering. She tentatively approached Brit and didn't flinch when he patted her neck. Then, as Brit went on talking to her, she rubbed her nose against his chest.

A moment later Pete and Bob climbed up onto the ledge.

Jupe introduced them. "Pete Crenshaw and Bob Andrews, this is Brit. . ."

"Douglas," Brit finished. "Hi. Glad to know you."

Pete and Bob smiled. They now understood those crazy calls. They had mistaken Brit's voice for Jupe's.

"I guess you could all use a drink of water," Brit said. "Come on. I'll take you to my hideout."

Holding Blondie's bridle, he led the way along the ledge and then up a twisting path. At the top they came to a half-hidden opening in the face of the mountain.

"Keep your heads down," Brit warned as they followed him into a narrow tunnel. "Okay. You can straighten up now."

Only a little light filtered in through the tunnel, but the Three Investigators could see they were in a large cave with a high ceiling.

Brit struck a match and lit a candle. Jupe guessed Brit had been living here for some time. A sleeping bag was rolled up on the floor. Pots and pans, a kerosene cookstove, some half-filled sacks, and several picks and shovels were stacked around the walls. From the look of the smooth ceiling, he could also tell no gunpowder had ever exploded in here. This couldn't be Pancho Villa's cave.

Brit picked up a sack and emptied a heap of oats onto the floor. "Good thing Dad got these for his horses," he said. "There isn't much to graze on around here. Even for a hungry burro."

Bob was looking at the single sleeping bag.

"Where *is* your father?" he asked.

"Why? Why do you want to know?" Brit's eyes were suddenly wary again.

"Because we should warn him about Dusty too," Bob said.

Brit picked up a clay jug and poured some water into a pan for Blondie.

"No. Dad took the horses down to the valley to get supplies." He handed the jug to Pete and all three Investigators took a quick refreshing drink from it.

"He's gone down toward the lake?" Jupe asked. "I hope he doesn't run into Dusty."

"No. He didn't go that way. There's a village on the other side of the mountain. It only has a couple of stores and Dad won't be able to find what we need there. The village doesn't even have a vet. But the bus stops there, the bus to . . ."

Brit stopped and looked at the guys as though trying to make up his mind if he could trust them or not.

"Why did you come up into the mountains?" Brit asked.

"It was Dusty's idea . . ."

The time had come to tell Brit the whole story. Jupe explained about the crossword contest with answers that had to be tape-recorded. How he and his friends had finally realized what it was all about—Pancho Villa's silver pesos.

Brit had listened in silence until then, sitting with the Three Investigators, on the ground.

Now he suddenly stood up.

"Dusty told you about the silver?" he asked furiously. "What did he do? Promise you a share if you found it?"

"No," Pete assured him. "Dusty never let on about that. His story was that we were going up into the mountains to file down Blondie's hooves."

"What!"

Pete went on, "Mercedes was the one who told us about Pancho Villa."

"Mercedes?" Brit frowned in a puzzled way. "Who's Mercedes?"

Bob described her. Her long black pigtails. Her dark eyes.

"She's Mexican?" Brit was still frowning.

"Seems to be," Jupe said. "I've never heard her speak anything but Spanish. And her skin's brown."

He was getting a little puzzled himself now.

"Mercedes told us to warn you about Dusty. She said she was a close friend of yours. You know her, right?" Pete asked.

Brit shook his head.

"I've never heard her name," he said. "And as far as I know, I've never seen her in my life."

12

A Shaky Situation

"THESE HILLS ARE FULL OF CAVES," BRIT SAID. "Pancho Villa and his men probably used most of them as hideouts. But Dad's sure we've found the one where he hid those silver pesos."

The four guys were sitting on their rolled sleeping bags in Brit's cave that evening. He had cooked up a big pot of their favorite—beans and rice—on the kerosene stove. Three candles were burning now and Brit had hung a blanket over the entrance to the tunnel so no light would show outside. Blondie was contentedly nibbling at her oats in a corner.

"How do you know you've found the right cave?" Pete asked. "If this place is so full of them."

"Well, for one thing," Brit explained, "the entrance was all blocked up with fallen rocks. And when we managed to shift some of them, we found Ignacio."

"Ignacio?"

"One of Villa's soldiers," Brit explained. "Of course, he wasn't in very good shape after being buried under tons of rocks since 1916. Just a skeleton with pieces of uniform sticking to him. And his skull—"

"Do you mind?" Pete interrupted him. "I'm trying to eat."

Bob smiled. "Dead bodies put Pete off his feed."

"Oh, don't worry, we gave him a decent funeral." Brit laughed. "Dad put up a cross over his grave and carved the name Ignacio on it in memory of one of Mexico's great military heroes. Ignacio Allende was, well, like their George Washington and—"

"Did you get inside the cave yet?" Pete still wanted to change the subject.

Brit shook his head. "We shifted some of the rocks with picks and shovels. But we couldn't get any farther. To where the silver is. That's why Dad took off. To buy explosives."

"When do you think he'll be back?" Jupe asked.

"Not for three or four days. It's only a few hours' ride down to the village. Dad'll leave the horses there to get a good feed and a rest. He'll need them both to carry back all the supplies. And then he'll take a long bus ride to Chihuahua. That's the nearest town where he can buy the dynamite and other things we need."

"So that leaves the four of us to handle Dusty. And maybe Mercedes," Bob said. "I guess a quartet ought to be able to manage this gig. If we all play together."

Brit looked at his new friends. "I'm glad I won't have to do it solo," he said. "I want to tell you it was great of you to come and warn me about Dusty. I mean, you didn't even know me."

"Well. . ." Jupe realized he hadn't told Brit who

they were. "It wasn't just you. We were on a case. So we wanted to follow through on it."

"What do you mean?" Brit didn't understand. "You sound like private eyes or something."

"That's what we are," Jupe told him. "Private investigators." He took a card from his pocket and handed it to Brit. It said:

THE 3 INVESTIGATORS
"WE INVESTIGATE ANYTHING"
Jupiter Jones, Founder
Pete Crenshaw, Associate   Bob Andrews, Associate

Brit looked at the card for a long time. He frowned and then began to read aloud in a slow, groping way.

"The three nivetsitagors," he said. "The three. . ."

He handed the card back to Jupe. "I guess you'd better read it to me," he said.

Jupiter didn't need to look at the card. He recited what was on it aloud.

"Oh." Brit looked shyly away at Blondie. "It isn't that I don't know how to read," he explained. "It's just that I have dyslexia. You know what that is?"

"Sure." Bob nodded sympathetically. "It means you see letters or words in the wrong order. They've been doing a lot of experiments on it lately, using colored lenses."

"Yeah. My mom wants me to see a specialist about that when I get home. But right now it's kind of hard for me to read or write letters. What we usually do is tape messages and mail each other cassettes when I'm away from her."

Jupe didn't say anything. The computer in his head was scrolling back—fast.

Another piece in the puzzle had just fallen into place. That tape he had found in his mailbox. "Please don't come to Mexico. You'll be in terrible danger. . ."

It must have been Brit's voice on that tape. Maybe part of a longer message he had sent his mother. She or someone else had erased all but a few sentences, then placed the cassette in the Joneses' mailbox. A warning to him. And a clue.

He smiled at Brit. "Is your mother in Los Angeles now?"

"Yeah. I sure hope so. But she's awfully stubborn and . . ." He looked away again as though he didn't want to say any more.

Jupe hated to press him. But there was one other thing he had to find out.

"Do you look like your mother?" he asked. "Does she have blond hair like you?"

"Yeah, she does. She has blue eyes like me too. Why?"

"Just wondering." Jupe yawned and stretched. "What do you say we all hit the sack?"

The others agreed. A few minutes later they had blown out the candles. The blanket over the entrance to the cave had been taken down and the four guys were in their sleeping bags.

When Jupe woke up early the next morning a faint light was seeping in through the tunnel from outside. He looked around for Blondie. She wasn't in the cave.

He scrambled out of his sleeping bag and went to search for her. He saw her at once about twenty yards away at the foot of the path that led up to the cave. As Jupe watched, she raised her head and brayed. She didn't sound wary, just friendly. A moment later he heard an answering bray from farther down the mountain.

Mercedes' burro, he thought. He stepped quickly back out of sight behind a rock. A moment later Pete, Bob, and Brit joined him. They had heard the braying too.

The soft calls continued back and forth between Blondie and her invisible friend. Then the other burro appeared, climbing a steep gully. Blondie trotted forward and the two rubbed against each other.

Mercedes' burro still wore its rope bridle, but the packs were missing from its back. The sky grew brighter as the sun rose. All four guys looked carefully around in every direction.

They didn't see Mercedes.

"Let's take them both back into the cave," Pete suggested. "If Mercedes sees Blondie, she'll know we're around."

Brit and Jupe led the two burros inside. Pete and Bob followed.

"You don't trust Mercedes, do you?" Brit asked.

"She's another puzzle," Jupe admitted. "She did ask us to warn you about Dusty. But she also told us she was a close friend of yours. And you've never set eyes on her. As Bob says, she's one tricky lady."

Both burros were hungry. Brit fed and watered them as soon as they were safely hidden in the cave. Then Pete cooked up their usual breakfast of beans and rice. Jupe was beginning to look forward to salads again. They didn't all eat together. Jupe kept watch at the end of the tunnel while he had his breakfast. He lay flat on the ground, well out of sight, scanning the country below for any sign of Mercedes. The other guys would take turns, an hour at a time.

He felt it first in his chest. A slight trembling of the hard-packed earth. It was enough to make him drop his fork. He had lived through enough earthquakes in Los Angeles to know this wasn't like that. He didn't feel any sudden shock. This was more like standing on a sidewalk when a heavy truck rumbles by.

He told Bob about it when his friend relieved him on watch an hour later.

"Yeah," Bob agreed. "We felt it in the cave, too. Like the bass when the amps are turned up too high. These mountains can be mean. Hey, what's the deal on that forest fire we spotted yesterday?"

He turned and looked up behind him. But the

mountaintop was hidden by the sheer face of the cliff above the cave entrance.

"*Quién sabe?*" Jupe answered, and Bob took over the watch for Mercedes.

Two hours later Pete was on watch when he thought he saw something move way below him. He whistled a bird call to his friends in the cave.

"Where?" Jupe whispered as they all flattened themselves in the entrance to the tunnel.

"Down there." Pete pointed over to the left.

He didn't need to say any more. They could all see the distant figure now.

A man wearing a Stetson and carrying a long-barreled rifle was climbing slowly toward them.

Dusty.

13

Second-guessing

"THERE'S NO POINT HIDING IN THE CAVE," JUPE whispered. "Dusty will track us right to the tunnel. If he comes in shooting . . ."

"Maybe we could ambush him somehow," Bob suggested.

"Yeah." Jupe nodded. "I've got an idea that might work."

"Okay, spill it," Pete said softly.

"Let's get some privacy." Jupe was already crawling back into the cave. The others followed him.

A minute later Jupe, Brit, and Bob emerged. Brit crouched, holding his rifle across his chest. Waiting until Dusty had moved out of sight, he scrambled down the twisting path and disappeared among the rocks below. Bob quickly followed Brit and disappeared too.

Jupe remained lying in the entrance to the tunnel. Keeping his head down, he saw Dusty move out into the open. With his rifle ready, Dusty was climbing steadily, following Blondie's hoofprints.

Jupe waited until the rancher was less than twenty yards away.

"Dusty," he called. "Dusty, it's Brit."

"Brit?" Dusty's hand slipped up the stock of his rifle to the trigger. "Where are you, Brit?"

"Up here," Jupe called back. "And I've got my rifle aimed at you."

Dusty laughed. "Go ahead and shoot," he said. "I'll know exactly where you are then. And I'll blast you away."

He had reached the foot of the path. He kept on coming with his easy, loping stride.

"What do you want?" Jupe made his voice sound scared. "Why did you come here?"

"Just to talk. Have a friendly chat with you and your dad about Pancho Villa."

"Drop your rifle."

The real Brit stepped out from the rocks behind the rancher and prodded him hard in the back with the barrel of his gun. Dusty looked bewildered.

"Go on. Throw it on the ground," Brit ordered firmly.

Jupe's plan had counted on Dusty's surprise. One minute the rancher thought he was talking to Brit up ahead. The next minute he heard Brit's voice right behind him.

He didn't drop his rifle. But he was confused enough to lower it.

"Don't turn your head," Brit told him in the same firm voice.

Just as Jupe had hoped—that was exactly what Dusty did. At least he started to.

Bob leaped out of his hiding place.

Dusty had his head half-turned toward Brit. He never saw Bob coming. Before he could move, Bob grabbed the rifle out of Dusty's hands and threw it into a cactus bush ten yards away.

Snarling, Dusty turned on Bob.

Bob moved fast into a karate position. He wasn't as good a karate fighter as Pete, but he was strong and quick. He thought he could take Dusty if the man attacked him.

But Dusty didn't attack Bob. He suddenly whirled at Brit. His arm swung around with his body. He backhanded Brit hard across the head. Brit staggered back. Bob moved forward, but the rancher already had his hands on the barrel of Brit's rifle. A quick, strong twist and he wrested it free. Stepping back, he turned the gun on Bob.

Dusty sneered. "Okay, you jokers," he said. "Get going. Downhill. And don't stop until you're out of range."

Disarmed, there was nothing the two guys could do. If Brit made another move, Dusty would shoot Bob. They both started slowly down the trail. Dusty waited until they were a safe hundred yards away. Then he turned and started to climb toward Jupe again.

"Come on out, Fat Boy," he called. "Come on out or I'll start shooting."

Jupe stood up. Dusty's finger tightened on the trigger.

"Okay," he said. "You can go join your friends in a minute. But first I've got a couple of questions I want to ask you."

Jupe would have given anything to get a judo hold on the rancher. But with a gun aimed at his chest, he couldn't move close enough.

"Where's Brit's father?"

Jupe thought fast. He had to make Dusty believe there was no one in the cave.

"He and Pete went to get some water," he said.

"How come I didn't see them?"

"The spring's a couple of miles away. Around the other side of the mountain. You can't see it from here."

Dusty nodded slowly. He smiled. "So there's no one but you between me and Villa's loot," he said. "Fine. Now move your fat behind. Go and hide with your friends in those gullies down there. Just keep outta my sight. And if you don't want a bullet in your backside, move fast and keep going."

Jupe shrugged. Assuming a beaten, crestfallen look, he started quickly down the path.

Dusty watched him until he disappeared behind the rocks. Then he lowered his head and, holding the rifle in both hands, he started into the tunnel.

Pete heard him coming. He was waiting just inside the cave. He figured Dusty would enter with his head down. A perfect target for a karate chop.

He raised his arm. With his fingers rigidly extended, his hand was as lethal as a two-by-four. One strike across the back of the rancher's neck and he would drop to the floor unconscious.

Dusty emerged into the cave. Pete brought his arm down fast. But one of the burros made a slight noise and Dusty raised his head an instant too soon. The blow caught him across the shoulders. He stumbled forward. But he didn't drop the rifle.

Pete was after him at once. He had his hand raised ready to strike again. But as he had shown outside with Bob and Brit, Dusty's reflexes were trigger fast. He stepped back. The gun came up, pointed straight at Pete. Pete lowered his arm.

He figured he had one advantage against that rifle. Dusty had just come in out of the sunlight. Pete's eyes had grown used to the darkness of the cave. If he moved fast enough, he might be able to surprise Dusty before he could shoot.

He feinted to one side, then suddenly spun on the ball of his foot. His right leg shot out behind him. His foot caught the rancher just below the chest, knocking the wind out of him. Dusty doubled up for a second, gasping.

This time Pete had just the target he needed. Leaping forward, he brought his elbow down on the back of the rancher's neck.

The *otoshi-hiji-ate*, the downward elbow strike, did it every time. Dusty dropped to the floor. Out for the count.

He was still lying there unconscious when the other three guys joined Pete. Brit was handy with ropes and knots. He soon had Dusty trussed up like a steer at a rodeo. The four guys stood looking down at the helpless rancher. The two burros who had stood huddled together during the fight went back to their oats.

"Let's take ten," Bob said after a minute.

The four guys went outside.

"Okay, I know." Jupe smiled. "It didn't work out quite the way I planned. But Pete's lightning reflexes took up the slack."

Pete laughed and chopped the air. "These hands are registered weapons, you know."

"Oh, right," Bob said. "And my name is Bruce Lee. What's up next, Jupe?"

"First, let's get Dusty's rifle," Brit said. "Like heads, two guns are better than one."

They hurried down the path to the clump of cactus where Bob had thrown Dusty's rifle. They bent down, searching the stony ground.

They searched and searched. They went over every rock and crevice. They looked under every prickly cactus leaf.

The rifle was gone.

"Mercedes," Bob stated. "She's around here some-where. And now she's got Dusty's rifle."

Jupe was pulling at his lip. "I've got an idea," he said after a moment.

"Here we go again," Pete groaned. "More second-guessing?"

"I don't think Mercedes is hiding around here," Jupe went on thoughtfully. "I think she's gone back to her base."

"What base?" Pete asked.

"She unloaded those packs from her burro," Jupe reasoned. "So she's camped somewhere. And as Hector Sebastian told me, burros are faithful animals. They attach themselves to people. So if I take Blondie along to keep it company, Mercedes' burro might lead me to her camp."

"You?" Bob kidded him. "You want solo credit or something? Why don't we all go?"

"Because if there are four of us, she'll see us coming," Jupe told him. "If I'm alone I can keep out of sight behind the burros. You've got to admit I'm a lot thinner than I used to be. Harder to spot."

"You're not exactly as thin as Ignacio," Bob pointed out.

The others laughed. But Jupe's mind was elsewhere.

Jupe had a hunch about Mercedes. It was kind of a wild hunch. All he had to go on was her contact lenses and a glimpse of her wrist by the light of a campfire. But as an investigator, he knew hunches sometimes paid off. Maybe, just maybe that wasn't a scar he had seen when her watch had slipped down. The only way to test his hunch was to see Mercedes again at close range.

"Okay, you're on," Pete agreed. "But that woman's got a gun now. Keep your eyes open."

Brit brought the two burros out of the cave. "Dusty's

still tied up, hand and foot," he reported. "But his mouth's working fine. He told me exactly what he's going to do to us when he gets loose."

Jupe gave Mercedes' burro a slap on its rump and it set off willingly enough. Blondie walked beside it. Jupe kept both of them between himself and the rock face, stooping slightly to stay out of sight of anyone above him.

The burros didn't climb. They stuck to a more or less level trail around the mountain. Glancing up, Jupe could see entrances to other caves. But he couldn't see any tracks leading up to them. And Mercedes' burro kept going.

Without warning, it stopped.

Blondie halted beside it. Jupe flattened himself on the ground. A hundred yards above him was a cleft in the rock face. Taking advantage of every scrap of cover, he worked his way up toward it.

Mercedes' burro didn't follow him. But it didn't move on, either. Blondie had found a small clump of sagebrush. Both animals started grazing quietly.

Maybe I'm on the wrong trail, Jupe thought. Maybe that narrow opening in the cliff isn't the entrance to Mercedes' campsite. I'll get a little closer to it anyway, he decided.

Then a cold hand seemed to grip the back of his neck. He felt his scalp shiver.

There, not two yards from his face, something was sticking up from the ground. A rough wooden cross. Staring at it, Jupe could see the name carved on it.

IGNACIO.

So he'd found it! This was the entrance to the cave Brit and his father had discovered. The cave where Pancho Villa had hidden his silver pesos.

Had Mercedes found it too? Was that where she had made her camp?

Was she up there now?

If she was, she would probably have seen the two burros by this time. She would want to find out what they were doing there.

Jupe lay flat on the ground. Waiting.

He didn't have to stay there more than a minute. He saw the familiar figure of the Mexican woman in her loose woolen skirt, with her long black pigtails and purple shawl, step out of the cave and look down at the two burros.

He saw her cock the bolt of the rifle she was holding.

Go for it, Jupe prodded himself. It was time to find out the truth about Mercedes.

He kept his head down. Just in case he was wrong. Just in case she responded to his hunch with a rifle shot.

"Mom!" Jupe shouted. "Mother! It's me! Brit!"

14

Out of the Frying Pan

FOR THE LONGEST TEN SECONDS OF JUPE'S LIFE, Mercedes did not move.

Then she dropped the rifle and ran eagerly down the slope toward him.

"Brit," she shouted. "Brit, dear, where are you? Are you all right?"

She was no longer pretending she didn't speak English.

Jupe stood up. "Yes, Brit's fine," he called back. "I'm sorry I played that trick on you, but he needs your help. We all do."

Mercedes stopped a few yards away from him. For another ten seconds she stared at Jupe. Then she smiled at last.

"Quick," she said. "Come on up to the cave and tell me what's happened."

The two burros were still browsing contentedly. Jupe followed Mercedes up to the cleft in the rock face.

"Where's Dusty?" She picked up the rifle and looked carefully down the mountain.

"Don't worry about him." Jupe told her what had happened in Brit's hideout. "Brit's got him safely tied up."

She nodded, relieved, and slipped the safety catch back on the rifle. "I've been worried to death about Brit and Tom, my husband," she said. "I found this cave yesterday with some of their things in it. But there weren't any fresh horse tracks, so I didn't know where they'd gone."

Jupe explained that Brit's father had left to buy the dynamite they needed to blast their way through to Villa's treasure and would be back in a few days.

"How did you happen to find Dusty's rifle?" he asked.

"My burro strayed off during the night while I was sleeping," Mercedes told him. "This morning I went out to look for it. I couldn't find the burro but I saw this gun under a cactus. It has Dusty's initials on it. There was no other sign of Dusty and I was afraid it was a trap. I thought he might be hiding somewhere with another rifle. Or that knife he used to carry in his boot. So I hurried back here. At least I could see him coming from here."

Jupe smiled. Dusty hadn't been hiding when she found the rifle. He was being trussed up with Brit's expert knots. Mercedes had missed all the action by only a few minutes. From where Bob had thrown the rifle, she wouldn't have been able to see the entrance to Brit's cave. So she had missed that, too.

Mercedes was smiling again. "How did you guess I was Brit's mother?" she asked. "You've never heard me speak anything but Spanish before. And I don't look much like an American in this thing."

She lowered her shawl and tugged off the black wig with its pigtails. She stuffed it into her pocket. Then she ran her fingers through her own blond hair.

"It was really a hunch. A lucky hunch," Jupe explained. "But I did have a couple of things to go on. When we were talking by the campfire that night, your watch had slipped down your wrist. I saw a band of much lighter skin. . . ."

He held out his left arm. His skin had become deeply tanned on the trip. He unfastened the strap of his digital watch, exposing the white band on his wrist where the sun hadn't reached.

"Most Mexicans have brown skin," he went on. "Even if they tan on top of that, they wouldn't have a strip of dead-white skin under a watchband. But Anglos with pale skin could."

She nodded. "You're smart—just like my Brit."

"It wasn't only me. My friend Bob caught something too. Your contact lenses. Actors sometimes use them in movies to change the color of their eyes. So I had two hunches about you. Maybe brown wasn't the natural color of your skin. And maybe you didn't have a Mexican's dark brown eyes either."

"No, I don't." She ducked her head and slipped out the two lenses. "They're the same color as Brit's." She looked up again, showing her blue eyes. She put the lenses into a plastic case and slipped it into her skirt pocket.

"Besides, I've heard you speak English," Jupe reminded her. "Although I admit I didn't recognize your voice in Spanish. You called me at the ranch and asked me to meet you on the other side of the lake."

Brit's mother reached out and squeezed Jupe's hand. "I'm sorry about that. Ascención told me it was a stupid thing to do. But I didn't realize just how dangerous that lake is. I wasn't trying to kill you. Only hoping to scare you off—"

"To keep Blondie from leading me up here."

She nodded. "I was so frightened. I knew Dusty might kill Tom and Brit if he found them. He'd do anything to get his hands on those pesos." She paused. "I was so scared I did some other stupid things too. Paying that Mexican to try to keep you off the bus. Then trying to steal Blondie that night. I should have known she wouldn't let me near her."

She searched behind a rock and pulled out a walkie-talkie. Looping its strap over her shoulder, she picked up the rifle. "Now, please, take me to Brit's cave," she said. "I'm dying to see him."

"Have you managed to contact Ascención lately?" Jupe asked as they led the two burros back along the trail toward Brit's hideout.

"So you know about that too, Jupiter?"

"Well, Mercedes . . ." Jupe smiled. "I'm sorry, I don't know your real name."

"It's Grace. That's *merced* in Spanish," she said.

"Grace Douglas. You can go on calling me Mercedes if you like."

"Okay, Mercedes." Jupe went on. "I knew Ascención had a walkie-talkie. I fixed it for him at the ranch. And Bob spotted yours on the burro that night you came to talk to us."

She shook her head in a worried way. "I tried to call Ascención again and again this morning. But there was no answer. I did get through to him one night on the trip and he was only a day's ride behind me then. So he should have been here by now unless . . ." She hesitated, suddenly anxious. "Unless Dusty found him and killed him."

"Dusty knew Ascención was following him?"

"He must have guessed it. That's why he pretended his horse went lame. So he could keep circling back over his own trail. Watching for Ascención. Dusty wouldn't have worried about a Mexican woman on a burro if he saw me. But if he spotted Ascención up in these mountains, he'd kill him." She hesitated. "And maybe he has."

"Mercedes." Jupe touched her shoulder, trying to reassure her. "I wouldn't worry too much about Ascención. I know Dusty's smart. But Ascención is something else."

"Yeah." Mercedes nodded hopefully. "Yeah, he sure is."

As they hurried on, Jupe asked Brit's mother how she had come to suspect Dusty was planning to use Jupiter to find Villa's cave.

She was in close touch with Brit, she explained, sending tapes to him at the village on the other side of the mountain and receiving his taped answers in Los Angeles. So she knew the whole story about Blondie's blindness and the long trek to Dusty's ranch for a vet. Brit had also warned her that the rancher might try to use the little burro to find Brit and his father in the mountains.

Then she received a letter from Ascención, saying Dusty was planning to go to L.A. Ascención enclosed a copy of the crossword puzzle that Dusty had had printed in Lareto. The Mexican hadn't understood what the puzzle was all about. But he knew Dusty was up to something.

"Well, I didn't figure it all out at once," Mercedes went on, "but I did know who Dagwood's wife was: Blondie. So I started watching that store where the contest entries were sent. It wasn't long before Dusty showed up there to collect his mail. I tried to break into the store the next day. But the burglar alarm scared me off."

After that she kept a close watch on the rancher and found out where he was staying. Then one day she followed him out to The Jones Salvage Yard. Driving slowly past the house, she saw Dusty talking to Jupe on the porch. She hid her car and crept back to the house.

"I could hear you talking," she said. "And what struck me at once was your voice. It was just like Brit's!"

So she had started to fit things together. Disguising herself as a Mexican, she followed Jupe and his two friends to Lareto.

"I saw Dusty pick you up there in his Jeep. So I moved into a room in the village on the other side of the lake and got in touch with Ascención again. I spied on you in the woods. And when Blondie made friends with you right away, well, it wasn't hard to figure out the rest."

They walked on for a while in silence.

"Do you mind if I ask you a couple of questions?" Jupe asked.

"Go ahead."

"How do you know Ascención? And what happened between you and Dusty that made you—"

"That made us hate each other so much?"

"Yeah."

"It goes back a long way," Mercedes told him. "My mother died when I was a child. My father was a mining engineer working for a Mexican company. I was brought up in Mexico. Ascención used to take care of me as a kid when my father was away on mining trips. In those days Ascención owned the whole ranch. He was doing fine, raising cattle and horses until Dusty came along—"

"And took over the ranch from him." Jupe remembered those deeds he had seen in Dusty's office.

"Yes. Like most ranchers, Ascención owed money to the bank. And Dusty bought up the notes on the loans. Before Ascención could sell enough cattle to settle his debts, Dusty foreclosed on everything. I went to court to try to help my old friend. But Dusty knew the right people to pay off. In the end Ascención lost the ranch to him."

Jupe looked down into the valley and across to the next range of mountains. He hoped Mercedes was wrong and Ascención would show up soon.

But there was no sign of him.

And then Jupe felt a sudden blast of heat. Without warning the air, the whole land around him changed.

It grew hotter. And darker.

Looking up, he saw a great gray cloud spread across the sky. He felt that shivering of the earth again. He could see the mountaintop from where he was now. A jet of dark smoke was shooting up out of it. A jet far thicker and heavier than any of those white plumes he had seen before.

Suddenly he understood. He could have kicked himself for being so dumb. Why hadn't he realized the truth earlier? Pete had even wondered why the white smoke didn't hang about in the air. That wasn't smoke—it was steam.

"It's a *volcano*," Jupe said in a choked voice.

Mercedes clutched his arm, pulling him to a stop. Shielding her eyes with her hand, she looked up at the mountain too.

"Yes," she whispered. "I never knew there were any active volcanoes in the Sierra Madre. But I've seen them in Hawaii. And this one's about to explode!"

15

All Tied Up

"I'M INTO ROCK MUSIC IN A BIG WAY," BOB TOLD BRIT. "Really into it. But some of those stars can be a pain in the neck."

The three of them—Bob, Brit, and Pete—were sitting around in the cave, waiting anxiously for Jupe.

The tension was so thick you could pierce it with a pickaxe. Bob and Brit chattered on as if they didn't notice. But they wondered to themselves how long they could keep the desperate rancher under control. The man kept struggling against his bonds and yelling.

"I'm into rock too," Brit said. "And I can't be*lieve* you really know guys like the Survivors."

"Sure, they hang around the office all the time."

"But Mexican music is hot too," Brit said. "Does your boss handle any Mexican singers?"

Bob shook his head. "Latin music is a whole other scene."

Pete, who had heard Bob's pop music stories until he was blue in the face, was writing a long letter to Kelly Madigan.

"Dear Kelly," he wrote, "It's really wild in the mountains. Right now I'm sitting in a cave with a guy who's tied up with ropes. No, we're not into whips and chains up here, but . . ."

Pete threw down his pad and glanced at his watch. "It's over two hours since Jupe left," he said. He crawled to the end of the tunnel to look for him again.

Dusty wasn't writhing around anymore. He was kneeling on the floor. Trussed up the way he was, he obviously found kneeling more comfortable than lying down.

"Hey, Brit," Dusty called in a croaking voice. "Bring me a drink of water, will you? My throat's so dry I can't swallow."

Brit and Bob exchanged questioning looks. Bob nodded.

"Sure." Brit picked up the clay water jug and carried it over to the rancher.

From where he was sitting, Bob couldn't see what happened next. One moment Brit was holding the jug to Dusty's lips. Then it shattered on the floor and Brit was lying on his back. The rancher was holding the sharp point of a sheath knife against Brit's neck.

Dusty's hands and feet were free. The cut cord dangled from his wrists.

"You idiots." He laughed in a wild, gloating way. "You should have had the brains to search me. I always carry a knife in my boot."

He pressed the blade against Brit's throat, threatening his jugular if he made a move.

"Okay, Bob," Dusty called in the same jeering voice. "Bring me Brit's rifle. Go on. Move it."

Bob knew the rancher wouldn't hesitate to cut Brit's throat. The rifle was leaning against the wall. He picked it up and walked over to Dusty.

"Drop it there. Where I can reach it."

Something in Dusty's voice made Bob's blood freeze. Dusty wasn't just willing, he was eager to use the knife on Brit. Bob dropped the rifle.

Still holding the knife against Brit's jugular, Dusty picked up the rifle and cocked it.

"Now go face the wall, Mr. Big Shot. And put your hands on your head."

"No sign of Jupe. But there's something real weird . . ."

Pete had returned through the tunnel. It took a second for his eyes to adapt to the dim light. Then he saw Bob standing face to the wall with his hands locked together across his head.

"What's going on . . ." he began. Then he saw Dusty. The crazed rancher was sitting astride Brit's chest, the threatening knife in one hand and the rifle in the other. His finger was on the trigger. The barrel was aimed at Pete.

"He faked us out," Bob explained. "He had a knife in his boot."

"You! Up against the wall too!" Dusty shouted at Pete.

For a wild moment Pete thought of rushing the rancher. Firing the rifle with one hand, Dusty might miss him in the half-darkness.

But there was no way Pete could reach Dusty before he sliced that gleaming blade across Brit's throat. Pete turned and faced the wall beside Bob.

"What do we do now?" Pete whispered.

"Hang tight till Jupe gets back," Bob whispered back.

"Hands on top of your head and shut up," Dusty shouted at Pete. "Serve you right if I plugged you both." He laughed viciously.

Pete did as he was told. He heard the creak of the rancher's boots as the man got to his feet.

Dusty slipped the knife into his belt and clasped the rifle in both hands. "Now you." He glanced down at Brit and gave him a kick in the ribs. "Get up and do what I tell you. Or you'll lose your two new friends."

Brit stood up. Unlike Pete and Bob, he had no training in karate. No defense against that rifle.

"Get back, Brit."

Brit backed toward the wall where the other two guys were standing.

"Hold it. Now get this straight, Brit. I'm not going to shoot you—yet. Tell me what I want to know or the other two'll get it in the back. *Comprende*, amigo?"

Brit nodded silently.

"Where's your father?"

Brit hesitated. He saw Dusty's finger tighten on the trigger.

"He went down to the village on the other side of the mountain."

"When'll he be back?"

For an instant Brit wanted to lie. But if Dusty guessed he wasn't telling the truth, one of the guys would pay for it with his life.

"Not for a couple of days yet," he said.

"Did you find Pancho Villa's cave?"

"Yeah."

"How do you know you got the right one?"

"We found the skeleton of one of Villa's soldiers buried under the rocks."

"Now you're talking. Get some rope and tie up these two guys the way you tied me."

Brit walked over to the far wall of the cave and came back with a length of heavy cord.

"You, Pete," Dusty ordered. "Down on your knees and put your hands behind your back."

Pete stalled for an instant. Dusty strode forward and jammed the muzzle of the rifle against the back of his neck. Pete felt the cold steel against his skin. He swallowed hard.

"Move it," snapped Dusty.

Swearing to himself, Pete knelt on the floor. He held out his hands behind him.

Brit tried to fake it at first. But Dusty was too close to him, watching and testing every loop of the cord around Pete's wrists and ankles, and then Bob's.

"Now I want some answers," Dusty told them.

"Actually, we're all tied up at the moment," Bob quipped.

Pete and Brit couldn't help snorting.

"Cut the clowning." Dusty prodded Bob sharply with the rifle. Bob's eyes blazed with anger, but he said nothing.

"Where did your pal go? The fat one."

"Wish we knew," Pete answered. "Maybe he went out for some pizza."

Brit watched Dusty's face darken. One of the guys was going to get himself blown apart if Dusty didn't get some real answers soon. "He went to find Mercedes," he put in quickly.

"Who's Mercedes?"

"We don't know," Brit answered truthfully. "She's a Mexican woman." He described her the way Bob had described her to him. "Jupe said she's been following them for days. And this morning we saw her burro outside. So Jupe took Blondie to try to track her to her hiding place."

"Has she got a gun?"

Brit thought quickly. He didn't have to admit he guessed she did. "Not as far as I know," he said.

"Okay. I'll keep a lookout for her. Black hair and pigtails." Dusty shifted the rifle from Bob and aimed it at Brit. "Now you're going to take me to Villa's cave. Go on. Move it. And don't forget I'm right behind you."

Pete heard the scraping of footsteps as Brit walked out through the tunnel, followed by Dusty.

As soon as the sound of footsteps died away, the two Investigators started struggling against the cords.

"Can you get your hands free?" Pete asked.

"Not without some help from Houdini," Bob said. "How about you?"

"No way."

"Where the heck is Jupe?" Pete asked.

"He'll be here," Bob promised. "You know that guy always has a scheme up his sleeve. He'll spot Dusty before that maniac can get close enough to shoot. Besides, Jupe's got Blondie. She can gallop a lot faster than Dusty can run."

"Dusty's not our only headache," Pete said, straining at the cord again. "You smell anything?"

Bob sniffed. "Rotten eggs?"

"Something weird's going on outside," Pete said. "When I was just out there, I couldn't see Jupe. I couldn't see *anything*. The whole mountain's as black as midnight. The air smells like . . . yeah, rotten eggs. And this huge cloud of smoke's spreading around."

Bob thought fast. "We saw smoke from this mountain before, remember? And that's not eggs," he cried, "it's *sulfur*! Like from a volcano. Holy smoke! We're sitting under a live volcano!"

Pete's eyes bulged. "We've got this cave to protect us. But Jupe's out there in the open!"

16

Rivers of Death

"GET DOWN," JUPE WHISPERED URGENTLY. "QUICK. Get down."

Mercedes was staring at the dark smoke that spurted from the mouth of the volcano and blanketed the mountain like fog. Jupe grabbed her by the arm and pulled her down behind a boulder.

"What is it?" she asked.

"Dusty," he whispered. "Keep your voice low."

Some gritty ash fell from the sky, but the wind was blowing the dark smoke away. A chemical smell hung in the air. Cautiously raising his head, Jupe watched the rancher. He was less than half a mile away, striding along the trail toward them. He wasn't alone.

Brit was walking a few steps ahead of him. The young guy's hands were clasped behind his neck. Dusty had his rifle aimed at his back.

"Brit." Mercedes drew in her breath sharply. Jupe had to grab her arm again to stop her from rushing forward to help her son.

"Don't," he warned her softly. "It won't help Brit if Dusty shoots you."

Any second now, Jupe thought, Dusty would see the two burros. He would have seen them before if he hadn't been watching Brit so closely.

Mercedes was sliding the rifle toward her. "I'll try to get Dusty in the arm," she whispered. She fitted the stock against her shoulder. She eased the barrel around the edge of the boulder. For a second she had a clear line of fire at the rancher.

She took careful aim. Her finger tightened on the trigger. She squeezed it.

Jupe waited for the sound of the shot. It never came. Mercedes was tugging and tugging at the trigger. She couldn't move it.

"The safety catch!" Jupe whispered. "The safety's on!"

Hastily Mercedes slipped it off. She aimed again. But now she was too late. Dusty had seen the two burros. He jumped forward and seized Brit from behind, shielding himself with Brit's body.

Mercedes lowered the rifle. She swore softly in Spanish. Dusty pulled the knife from his belt. He pressed it against Brit's back. Pushing Brit in front of him, he moved forward again.

Jupe snatched the strap of the walkie-talkie from Mercedes' shoulder. He flipped the switch to send.

"Ascención!" He held his lips close to the mike. "Ascención. Can you hear me?" he demanded in Spanish. "Ascención. Come in. Over."

He switched to receive. Silence. Jupe kept trying for another minute. Dusty was less than a hundred yards away now. He was still moving steadily forward, prodding Brit with the knife.

Jupe put the walkie-talkie down. He touched Mercedes' hand.

"Put on your wig."

She took it from her skirt pocket and quickly slipped it onto her head.

Dusty came to a stop ten yards away.

"Come out, Mercedes," he called in Spanish. "Come out where I can see you."

She didn't move.

"Don't be scared," Dusty went on, still in Spanish. "I know you're there. My friend here told me all about you. I know you followed us up here. And I bet you've got my rifle. Okay. No sweat. Maybe we can make a deal."

Mercedes stood up, holding the rifle in both hands.

Jupe stayed low. The rancher had somehow managed to get the jump on Pete and Bob. Probably with that knife he was holding against Brit's back. But as long as Dusty didn't know he was there, Jupe had the advantage of surprise. He might still manage to tackle the rancher.

Mercedes had her finger close to the trigger of her rifle.

"I know who you are too," she said in Spanish. "Señor Rice. And you are after Pancho Villa's silver."

"Right, señora," Dusty admitted. "And so are you."

"Okay." Mercedes nodded. "But I know where it's hidden. And you don't."

"Sure I do." Dusty moved closer. "This young American and his father found it. And now he's taking me there."

"If he thinks he knows where it is, he's wrong," Mercedes said. "He only knows where it *was*. Where I found it yesterday. But I used my burro to move it to another hiding place. Put your knife away. Then maybe, as you say, we can make a deal."

"Okay." Dusty slipped the knife back into his belt. "Now we're even. We've both got a rifle. But if you want to get that silver away from here, you're going to need my help." He glanced up at the mountaintop. "That thing's going to blow any minute now."

He was still moving slowly forward, holding Brit as a shield between himself and Mercedes.

"Stop where you are!" Mercedes shouted at him in Spanish. But she had realized the danger too late.

Dusty was staring at her. He sneered.

"You!" he spit out in English. "You fooled me for a minute in that Mexican wig. But I'd know those blue eyes anywhere, Grace."

Mercedes had forgotten to replace her contact lenses.

And then things happened so fast they all seemed to happen at once.

Mercedes started to raise her rifle. Dusty stepped quickly aside. He aimed at Mercedes.

Jupe heard a shot.

The rifle leaped out of Dusty's hand. It landed on the rocks five yards away. Dusty clasped his hand in pain.

Jupe jumped forward and snatched the knife out of Dusty's belt.

He heard the sound of clattering hooves. Ascención galloped up. He was holding a Colt .45 in his hand. He leveled it at Dusty.

"Next time I won't aim for your rifle. I'll aim for your heart," he said in Spanish. He glanced at Mercedes. She had her rifle pointed at Dusty. This time the safety catch was off.

"No," Ascención told her sharply. "Let him go. If you kill him, we won't have time to bury him. And that's a sin. To leave a body to the vultures."

He turned back to Dusty. "Get out of here!" he shouted at him. "Go find your silver."

Dusty was still clutching his hand. He hesitated, his face dark with hatred.

"Go," Ascención ordered him again. "Go to Pancho Villa's cave. You won't need Brit to take you there. You'll find enough tracks leading to it."

The rancher faced Ascención for a second. Jupe could see murder in his eyes. But Dusty was helpless. The breech of his rifle had been shattered when the Mexican shot it out of his hands. Jupe was holding his knife. He turned and set off along the trail that led to Villa's cave.

Mercedes and Brit hugged each other. Ascención dismounted. "That stupid walkie-talkie," he said. "I dropped it last night and I can't get a sound out of it."

Jupe looked up to the top of the mountain. Another plume of black smoke was rising.

"We've got to get Pete and Bob," he said. "They must still be in Brit's cave. We've got to get them out of there."

Ascención put two fingers into his mouth and gave a piercing whistle. A moment later another horse came cantering toward him. Jupe recognized it as Dusty's.

"I found her tethered down there," Ascención explained. "Now let's get out of here. Fast."

Jupe mounted Blondie while Mercedes straddled her own burro and Brit leaped onto Dusty's horse. With Jupe leading, they hurried off to Brit's hideout.

They were a hundred yards from the cave when Jupe felt something sting his face. And then his hand. Shading his eyes he looked up.

It was hailing!

Hailstones the size of match heads were falling from the sky. One landed on his shoulder. He plucked at it. He couldn't pry it loose from his T-shirt. Squinting at it, he saw it wasn't hail. It was a tiny bead of glass, as hot as a drop of boiling water.

What was going on up on the mountaintop? Jupe couldn't see. But it was trouble, for sure.

Urging Blondie to go faster, Jupe heard the two horses break into a gallop behind him. A minute later they all reached the shelter of the cliff face and drew to a halt.

Ascención grabbed the blanket that was folded under his saddle. He pulled out his knife and began slashing at it, cutting the blanket into strips.

"Go and look for your friends," he called to Jupe.

Jupe crawled into the tunnel. Pete and Bob were lying back to back, curled up on the floor. Pete had just managed to unfasten one of the knots binding Bob's ankles. He was working on Bob's wrists. Jupe quickly cut both of them free with Dusty's sheath knife.

"I thought you went out for pizza," Pete said, stretching the stiffness out of his arms and legs. "So where is it?"

Bob was stretching too. He stared at Jupe's head. "Is that the new *in* thing?" he asked. "Wearing glass beads in your hair?"

Jupe ran his hand over his head, trying to dislodge the beads. They were cool now, but he couldn't comb them out with his fingers. "It's hailing hot glass out there," he said. "Come on, guys. Let's move it!"

The three guys ran back out through the tunnel. The rain of glass had stopped for the moment. Ascención handed them long strips of blanket. "Tie these over your heads," he said. "Try to protect your arms and hands too." His own head and Brit's were already covered. Mercedes had spread her shawl over her face and shoulders.

"Okay. We go," Ascención shouted. Even Pete understood the *vamos*. He quickly mounted behind Brit. Bob vaulted up behind Ascención.

This time the Mexican led the way. Urging his horse down the twisting path, he headed for the valley below. When they reached the gullies that cut between the rocks, they snaked on down them as fast as they could. They could hear a low rumbling behind them now. It sounded like distant thunder. The smell of sulfur was so thick they could hardly breathe.

And then it happened. They were less than half a mile from the cave when the volcano erupted with a roar.

A great fountain of red-hot lava shot up from the mountaintop, then fell back. More fountains rose, higher and higher, like fireworks. Lava bombs rocketed out of the crater with deafening booms. They pounded the mountain slopes, spraying molten rock wherever they landed.

The roaring red geysers on top blasted hundreds of feet into the air, arced over, spilled lava down the mountainside. Streams of lava flowed, met, joined. They formed burning rivers. The rivers cascaded over the cliff face and into the gullies below.

Hot cinders began to rain down on the fleeing people, along with more burning glass beads. The hail of lava debris startled the unprotected horses and burros. Ascención's horse suddenly reared on its hind legs. It plunged and kicked so hard even Ascención could barely control it, and Bob had to tighten his arms around the Mexican's waist.

"Bring up Blondie," Ascención yelled.

Jupe spurred the burro into a canter.

"Between the horses!" Ascención shouted. "She'll calm them."

Jupe took a breath, then raced Blondie forward into the narrow gap between the two terrified animals. Gradually the horses settled down. As Blondie trotted on, they followed her.

The shower of burning hail thinned in a gust of wind. Jupe choked on a blast of sulfur, then held his blanket headdress in front of his mouth and nose. He had never trusted the outdoors. And now he knew he'd been right not to. How could they ever get out of here alive?

Bob looked back. Those rivers of red-hot lava were oozing closer and closer. Birds and small animals fled before the molten rock. Bushes burst into flame without even being touched. Bob heard a strange, crackling sound like shattering glass as the rivers approached.

This is it, he thought.

"At least we're going out in style," he said to Pete.

"Right," Pete answered. "Not everyone gets bleeped by a volcano."

The two of them stared back at the mountain. The heat from the onrushing lava stung their eyes, but they forced themselves to keep looking.

The sound of shattering glass grew louder. Bob felt a sudden surge of hope. A black crust was forming over those deadly rivers. They were no longer pouring down the slope. They slowly staggered forward, then paused. They lurched on another few yards and finally halted.

Then the shower of hot cinders and beads came to a stop too, falling short of the fleeing horses and burros.

They were safely out of range of the exploding volcano at last!

Half a mile farther on they reached the valley. Ascención led them quickly up the foothills of the next mountain range. There they halted.

They were all coughing from the poisonous fumes they had ridden through. They raised their heads and took deep gulps of fresh air. Then they turned and looked back at the volcano.

Ascención saw him first. He raised his arm and pointed. A distant figure was leaping desperately from rock to rock. It stumbled and scrambled upright again, racing away from Villa's cave.

On that side of the mountain the oncoming lava had only just reached the top of the cliff face. It seemed to hang there for an instant. Then it cascaded down—a river of death.

By some trick of sound they heard it quite clearly, echoing off the roaring mountain—Dusty's terrified scream as he disappeared under the molten stream of lava.

All four of the young guys closed their eyes. Dustin Rice had been a ruthless crook. And maybe a killer. But they had known him, traveled with him, eaten his food. And none of them had ever seen a man killed before. It shook them deeply. They were still shivering as they opened their eyes.

Ascención crossed himself and murmured a prayer in Spanish.

"I warned you," he said at last, looking at Jupe. "I warned you there was danger in the mountains."

They rode on, keeping to the crest of the foothills. Mercedes drew level with Ascención.

"I'm sorry, old friend," she said. "If Tom and Brit had gotten that silver, you could have bought your ranch back."

"Who knows?" Ascención shrugged. "Perhaps my ranch will return to me anyway."

He smiled in his patient Mexican way.

"When my mother told me about Villa's cave," he went on, "she also told me no one would ever find those pesos. There were too many of Villa's dead soldiers guarding them."

He paused.

"And now they'll guard them forever."

17

Born to Be Wild

RIDING ON, OUT OF DANGER NOW, THEY CIRCLED for miles around the volcano. They were heading for the well-protected village beyond the foothills on the mountain's other side.

They didn't talk much. Even Jupe's mind was at rest for a change. The last pieces of the puzzle had fallen into place.

Mercedes had first learned about Villa's treasure from Ascención. His grandfather had been a soldier in Pancho Villa's army in 1916. Mercedes had promised her old friend she would share half the silver pesos with him if her husband and son found them.

The secret had been carefully kept from Dusty until Brit showed up at the ranch with the little blind burro. Then the rancher had overheard him tell Ascención that he and his father had discovered Villa's cave.

And Dusty had cooked up his scheme to use Blondie to find the treasure himself.

Jupe was still shocked by the rancher's violent death. But it was Dusty's own greed that had killed him. If he hadn't made that last desperate effort to get his hands on the pesos, he would still be alive.

They stopped at a creek to water the animals and let them graze for ten minutes. A few miles farther on Jupe heard a strange sound—the distant braying of countless burros. Blondie brayed in response and trotted eagerly forward. The sound grew louder as she emerged from the woods.

There, stretching across the hills, were miles of pasture land. And cantering, grazing, and mingling on those hills were more than a hundred wild burros.

Blondie came to a stop. Her long ears were standing up straight, twitching with excitement. She gave a high, loud bray. Jupe slid down from her back. He slipped off her bridle and patted her neck.

Blondie looked at him for a moment with her big soft eyes. She rubbed her nose against him as though thanking him for bringing her home. Then she trotted over to Brit, sitting on horseback, and nudged his foot. He bent down and patted her head.

And then she galloped happily away to rejoin her own wild kind.

Jupe climbed up behind Mercedes. The group pushed on. If they hurried, they would reach the village before dark. From there Brit could phone his father in Chihuahua. He could tell him that he and his mother were safe and that they and Ascención would wait for him in the village.

The next day the Three Investigators would take a series of buses back to Rocky Beach.

"I'll see you in L.A.," Bob, who was now riding with Brit on Dusty's horse, promised his new friend. "We'll hit some rock concerts, hang out with the guys in the groups."

"Super," Brit said. "And I know a couple of girls in L.A. Maybe we can double-date."

"Yeah, maybe." Bob had a feeling he was going to be busy with his own girlfriends when he got back.

Pete, who was riding with Ascención, was thinking of Kelly. He had told her he would be away at least two weeks. Would her heart be fonder after only ten days? At least she'd have had less time to forget him. And she *had* given him a T-shirt with her name on it.

Hey, Kelly, he thought. Wait till you hear about how I escaped from a *volcano*.

Jupe was thinking about beans and rice. He never wanted to see another bean or another grain of rice as long as he lived. He knew he'd lost a good ten pounds, but his taste buds were bored to death. He couldn't wait to taste his first tomato, lettuce, and pickle salad again.

But first he had to treat his friends and himself to a big juicy pizza. They all deserved it.

Pete glanced at Bob as he drew up beside him. The words on Bob's T-shirt couldn't be truer.

The Survivors.

After all they had been through in these mountains, the Three Investigators had certainly proved to be that.

Survivors.